I0623144

THE KRAKEN RISES

ERIC S. BROWN

SEVERED PRESS
HOBART TASMANIA

THE KRAKEN RISES

THE KRAKEN RISES

Twin beams of light pierced the darkness of the waters. The Hanson's headlights ran along the length of the walls of the trench as the two-man submersible slowly crept through it. The X-29 was a new class of submersible. She was a thing of beauty to Pitts. Her maneuverability far surpassed anything else he had ever piloted in the depths. The X-29 was also equipped with a sensor array that seemed like something straight out of science fiction.

"This place is amazing, isn't it?" Thomas smiled beside him in the X-29's pilot compartment.

"Glad you're enjoying the ride, Doc," Pitts said, smiling back. The trench was anything but beautiful to Pitts. Its scarred, jagged walls spoke volumes about how violent the Earth could be. Pitts wasn't a scientist. He was just a very well-paid pilot that loved his job.

"Do you know how old this trench is?" Thomas asked him, the excitement thick in his voice.

Pitts managed to keep from sighing and holding his fake smile in place.

"This trench is older than mankind," Thomas said. "Far, far older than I'd dare hope when we spotted it yesterday."

"I still don't know how you got Cheryl to give you the okay to come back out here," Pitts said. "We're all supposed to be packing up."

Thomas gave him a stunned look. "For all that Cheryl is an administrator these days, she still understands what a find like this could mean to us all."

"Because of those readings, right?" Pitts questioned him.

"Yes. Those readings." Thomas' gaze was fixed on the data coming in from the X-29's sensors. "If I am right about what they are, inside this very trench, Lewis, at its bottom, could be a lifeform older than anything ever encountered before."

Pitts laughed, quoting an old movie, "Not all aliens come from space, eh?"

Thomas apparently recognized the line. "There are no such things as monsters." He looked up from the data on the screen in front of him to give Pitts a troubled look. "This isn't a horror movie, Mr. Pitts."

Pitts wanted to point out the X-29's forward window at the grotesque things that passed for fish at these depths, but there weren't any around. In fact, he hadn't seen any signs of aquatic life at all since the X-29 had entered the trench. "I hope you're right, Doc." Pitts shrugged and changed the subject. "You got me a destination yet?"

Fingers flying over the controls in front of him, Thomas sent the coordinates where the strongest of the readings he was picking up were coming from over to Pitts' pilot station.

"You should have it now," Thomas answered.

"That's the bloody bottom of this trench, Doc," Pitts complained.

"According to her specs, the X-29 can handle the depth," Thomas said.

"I didn't say she couldn't," Pitts pointed out. "But that far down, we're not going to be able to retain contact with Alpha One."

"Cheryl and the ops staff are aware of where we are and where we're likely headed," Thomas reminded him. "And like I said, this isn't a horror movie, Pitts. We'll be fine. All the evidence I've collected thus far points to whatever is down there being dormant. It's likely been asleep since before the dinosaurs died out. I don't think us taking a look around is going to wake it up."

Pitts grunted. Thomas was calling the shots after all. They were going down to the trench's bottom whether he liked it or not. Refusing to do so could very well cost him his job.

"Course plotted," Pitts said. "I'm taking us in."

The X-29 shifted in the dark waters, aligning itself for a direct descent towards the bottom of the trench. Pitts kept her descent slow and cautious. Even as deep as she already was, it would take another full ten minutes to reach the bottom of the trench. And though the X-29 was built for exactly this type of exploration, the pressure would be constantly increasing on her hull. Pitts knew she could take it, but it pushed even the X-29 to her upmost limits.

As the X-29 descended, Thomas hit a key on his controls, putting the sounds he was listening to on speaker.

"Do you know what you're listening to?" Thomas asked.

The noise reminded Pitts of a heartbeat. It was impossibly slow to be one though. The slow thud-thud-thud of the noise creeped him out. He wasn't about to admit that to Thomas however.

"Sounds like a heartbeat," Pitts answered.

"We can only hope so," Thomas said, beaming.

Suddenly, a new noise overpowered that of the heartbeat. It was high pitched like the cry of a dying cat. The noise was so intense that both he and Thomas clasped hands over their ears.

"Shut that off!" Pitts yelled at Thomas over the noise.

The shrieking continued to grow as the noise seemed to multiply. Instead of one cry, there were two and then dozens and then hundreds. Grimacing against the pain of the growing crescendo, Thomas managed to shut the speaker off.

Pitts' ears were ringing as he shouted, "What in the devil was that?"

Thomas had gone pale next to him. "I have no idea," Thomas answered.

An alarm light was flashing on the console in front Pitts. He blinked at it in surprise.

"What is that?" Thomas gestured at the alarm light.

"Do you want the bad news or the worse news?" Pitts asked as he cracked his knuckles and leaned over the X-29's helm controls.

Thomas merely stared at him.

"Well, we're not alone down here anymore, Doc," Pitts said bluntly. "And whatever is out there, they're closing on and us and fast. I suggest you get to work with the sensors and find out what it is that's coming at us."

The high-pitched cries had distracted Thomas from watching the data coming in from the X-29's sensor array. He saw now that a mass of *things*, clearly alive and mobile, had detached themselves from the lower walls of the trench. From what he could tell about their shapes, they reminded him of squids. They clearly weren't though. At least not any kind of squid he had ever seen in all the years of his career as a marine biologist before. They had characteristics of both squids and octopuses, but their bodies were far denser in terms of mass according to the readouts he was seeing. Each of them possessed eight tentacles that emerged from their lower bodies with two of those tentacles being thicker and much likely stronger than the others. Thomas swallowed hard.

"Mr. Pitts," Thomas said. "I think it's time for us to go."

"Couldn't agree with you more, Doc." Pitts was already in the process of bringing the X-29 about. She rolled in the water, her nose turning upwards towards the surface of the trench. As soon as she was in position, Pitts punched it. The X-29's engines howled in protest, straining, as the small craft shot upward, building speed as she went.

Pitts' had called up a tactical display on his screen, watching the creatures closing in on the X-29. Despite her increasing speed, the creatures were gaining on her.

"Just how fast can these things go, Doc?" Pitts demanded.

"They bare a strong resemblance to squids, Mr. Pitts," Thomas told him. "I think we should be able to outdistance them easily."

"Think again," Pitts growled, fighting with the X-29's controls and trying force power from her engines faster. "As far as I know, squids top out at around twenty-one knots, right?"

"Something like that," Thomas agreed, though Pitts was beginning to wonder just how shaken up he was. Thomas was nearly trembling in his seat, his eyes bugged out, and his skin pale.

"We're pulling thirty knots already, Doc and they're gaining on us," Pitts said. "Heck, Doc, tactical is placing the speed of those things at forty knots and climbing."

"That … That's impossible," Thomas protested.

"Tell them that," Pitts spat.

The X-29's engines topped out at their max speed of fifty knots as she cleared the mouth of the trench and continued to streak upwards towards the surface.

Both Pitts and Thomas were shaken in their seats as a large group of the creatures overshot the X-29, darting ahead of her, and the shockwaves of their wake washed over the craft.

"Mother …" Pitts started to curse, but his ability to form coherent words left him as he got his first look at the creatures through the X-29's forward window. There were roughly two dozen of the things ahead of the X-29 … and only God knew how many more behind it still chasing after them. Thomas was right about the things resembling squids. That was exactly what they looked like: misshapen and deformed squids.

Thomas had opened a channel to Alpha One. "This is X-29 Alpha. Mayday. I repeat. Mayday. We are under attack!"

"This is Alpha One," Cheryl's voice answered, sounding surprised and more than a little confused. "We hear you, X-29 Alpha, but did you just say you're under attack?"

Pitts could almost feel the level of disbelief she had to be experiencing himself. He couldn't blame her for feeling that way. The whole situation was utterly insane.

The creatures that had been shot by the X-29 swung about in the water and were heading around at it on a collision course. Pitts jerked the X-29 hard to port, dodging the bulk of them. One of the creatures made contact though. It ripped at the X-29's topside with its longer two tentacles. The screeching noise of them tearing at its hull echoed inside the submersible. Sparks flew from the damage the squid did to the craft, sending a power surge through the X-29's systems. Thomas recoiled in horror and panic, and the sensor station exploded, taking the X-29's comms with it. The doctor flopped from his seat onto the floor of the pilot compartment. If he had been in normal clothing other than a wetsuit, he likely would have been on fire and burning as he lay there.

The X-29 was so close to the surface. Just a little more and maybe, just maybe, they would make it, Pitts figured. If they reached the surface, the creatures might not follow them there, and even if they did, help would surely be on the way from Alpha One. The X-29 was a tough little vessel. Taking out her sensors and communications array was one thing, but tearing through her hull to get inside was an entirely other matter. Pitts knew the hull was designed to be impossibly strong. It had to be able to withstand the pressure of the depths it was built to explore. Even if the creatures attacked in mass, Pitts didn't think they would be able to tear through it before help arrived, if they could tear through it at all.

The creatures had closed in on the X-29. The sound of their thunder-like blows on the small craft's hull echoed around him. Thomas had managed to get himself together and grab a fire extinguisher, putting out the fire at his station. Flinging it aside, Thomas slipped back into his seat next to Pitts.

"They can't get in, can they?" Thomas asked in a strained voice.

Pitts chuckled darkly. "You're the scientist, man. You tell me."

Before Thomas could answer, one of the creatures slammed itself against the reinforced, specially made glass of the X-29's forward window. The squid-thing reared back its two primary tentacles, bringing them down onto the glass, again and again. Thomas cried out as the glass began to crack. Pitts started to send the small craft into a maneuver intended to shake the squid-thing off but never got the chance. The glass exploded inward, slicing through his flesh and the water outside followed it, filling up his lungs, as he opened his own mouth to scream.

****

The control room of the Alpha One platform was in chaos as Chief Dixon came charging into it. Alarm klaxons were blaring throughout the facility. Cheryl, the civilian head of the platform's crew, was standing over Peterson at the comm. station. She looked at him as he approached her.

"What in the holy freaking Hades is going on?" Dixon snapped.

"We've lost contact with the X-29 that Pitts took Thomas out in," Cheryl told him.

Dixon stared at her. "Weren't they heading to the trench?"

"It's more than just the usual comm loss that comes from something like that," Cheryl protested. "We received a mayday from them right before we lost contact. Thomas claimed they were under attack."

"Attack?" Dixon repeated the word. "Attacked by what?"

"How the hell would I know?" Cheryl asked, throwing up her hands in anger.

"Calm down," Dixon ordered her.

"Thomas sounded terrified out of his mind," Peterson said.

Dixon glared at the comm. tech. "That's not helping."

Peterson shrugged.

"Do we have the X-29's location?" Dixon asked.

Peterson nodded. "We're still picking up its locator beacon signal. She's surfaced five miles north of here."

"Tell Louis to prep the copter," Dixon ordered.

"Yes, sir," Peterson replied.

"Why did this have to happen now?" Cheryl complained. "Six months out here and not a single incident. Now two days from pick up and we've got all Hell breaking loose."

"You're the one who cleared Thomas' trip," Dixon reminded her.

"Come on, Dixon," Cheryl said, cheeks flushing red. "If he's right about what's at the bottom of that trench, it could be the find of our lifetimes."

"A new lifeform," Dixon commented.

Cheryl shook her head. "No, a very old one."

'Whatever." Dixon turned to Peterson. "I want the platform to remain on alert status until we get this mess figured out. Make sure Reece has medical ready too."

"Expecting the worst?" Peterson frowned.

Dixon didn't answer. Instead, he asked, "Do we have any video feed from the X-29?"

"The feed coming in before it just turned to snow and static was pretty distorted," Peterson said. "I could try to clear it up and play it back."

"Do it," Dixon ordered.

"It'll take a few minutes," Peterson told him.

"Louis says the copter is prepped and the rescue team is ready to go," Cheryl said.

However he might feel about Cheryl personally, Dixon had to admit the woman was dang good at her job. She was usually as by the book as bosses came. As Alpha One's head of security, technically, he outranked her in crisis situations like the one they were in now. Another boss might have let things slip some around the platform during the crew's long six-month stay but not Cheryl. Thanks to her, Louis and the rescue team had already been on standby when the X-29 left the platform.

Dixon felt helpless though he was doing everything he could. He imagined Cheryl felt the same only worse since she was the one Thomas had conned into giving him clearance to visit the trench. All either of them could do now though was wait and trust the rescue team to do their jobs.

The mention of an attack was certainly odd. Dixon could see that both Cheryl and Peterson were spooked by it. His first thought had been terrorists, and he still hadn't ruled that out. Dixon just couldn't imagine the X-29 meeting any sea life that could be a threat to it. The submersible was armored up tougher than a lot of tanks were. And it was fast too. With Pitts at its helm, anything going after it would be hard pressed to even get close enough to engage it, much less do it any serious damage. Something had happened though. He watched the screen that showed the X-29's current location. It wasn't moving. It was drifting, dead in the water.

"I've got the footage cleared up," Peterson said, waving at him.

He and Cheryl watched the final video stream from the X-29 over Peterson's shoulders.

Dark shapes moved through the water like bullets streaking towards the X-29. Even with the efforts Peterson had made to clear up the video, it was difficult to make them out.

"What are those things?" Peterson asked no one in particular then added, "They sort of look like squids."

"They're not squids," Cheryl said firmly. "Squids don't move like that."

Dixon didn't have a background in science like she did, but you didn't work security of places like the Alpha One platform and not pick up a few things over the years. "Squids aren't that fast," he agreed.

Dixon turned to Cheryl. "Do you think they were what Thomas was picking up down there?"

"I don't see how. Thomas showed me his data. It didn't point to anything like those creatures," Cheryl said.

"What did it point to?" Dixon asked, not sure he really wanted to hear her answer.

"Thomas thought there was a single, massive lifeform at the bottom of the trench." Cheryl frowned as she ran her fingers through her jet black hair.

"Frag," Dixon muttered. "And you gave him clearance to go anyway?"

"I agreed with him that whatever was down there had to be dormant, maybe in some kind of extended hibernation," Cheryl explained. "We both figured anything asleep that long wasn't going to be woken up by a brief visit from the X-29."

"I can see the logic in that, but clearly Thomas and Pitts stirred something up. Let's just hope they didn't pay too high a price for doing it," Dixon said.

"The copter is in route," Peterson cut in. "Louis says he has a visual on the X-29."

****

Louis could see the X-29 drifting in the water. The submersible's hull had taken a beating. Dents covered its surface. There were long gashes in the metal of the hull as well as if something had been clawing at it, trying to get inside. Louis understood why Alpha One had lost contact with the X-29. As badly damaged as its exterior was, he didn't doubt that the submersible's comm. and sensor array had been torn off it completely.

"This is Rescue 1," Louis said over the open channel to the platform. "I have eyes on X-29 Alpha. She's beat up pretty bad but appears intact. Commencing deployment of the rescue team."

"Hold off on that, Rescue 1," Cheryl's voice yelled into his ear through his headset. "Do you see any signs of activity in the water?"

"I'm sorry, ma'am," Louis paused, "say again?"

"You heard me, Louis," Cheryl growled at him. "Do you see anything in the water near the X-29? We have reason to believe it was attacked by … We don't really know what at this point. Squid-like creatures, very hostile and aggressive. Putting your team in the water may not be the best option in terms of how to proceed."

Louis bit his lip, wishing he had a cigarette. "There's no sign of anything down there but the X-29, ma'am. At least not that I can see from up here."

Had it been anyone other than Cheryl, he would have figured they were yanking his chain. Cheryl was always serious though. Louis turned in the copter's pilot seat to look into the rear section where Brandon and Nathan were standing, waiting on his order to go.

"The boss lady says there might be trouble in the water, boys," he told them. "Hold up for a second before you go down there."

"Can you get a winch onto the X-29, lift it out, and bring it back to the platform?" Cheryl asked.

"I think we can manage that, ma'am," Louis answered, "but I'm not seeing any kind of movement aboard the X-29 either. What if Thomas and Pitts...?"

"Thomas and Pitts are either safe inside the X-29 or dead," Security Chief Dixon answered him.

"Understood, sir," Louis replied, nodding his head slightly.

"And Louis," Dixon added, "don't let the rescue team touch the water. Hook up the wench from the air. Do you read me?"

"Loud and clear, sir." Louis watched the X-29 bobbing on the ocean's surface as he answered. "We'll haul her in A.S.A.P."

"What's going on?" Brandon asked, moving up to take the unmanned co-pilot seat. Teague, Louis's co-pilot, was back aboard Alpha One with a nasty stomach bug that had hit him out of the blue.

"Nothing good," Louis shook his head. "Alpha One says that getting in the water could be a very bad idea. They seem to think some kind of creatures did this to the X-29 and they might still be around here."

"Creatures?" Brandon laughed and then saw that Louis wasn't joking.

"Heard it straight from Cheryl herself," Louis assured him. "They want us to get a winch hooked up the X-29 and haul it home."

"That seems pretty extreme." Brandon looked through the copter's window at the X-29.

"You're telling me." Louis wanted to laugh but it didn't feel right. Not with the chance that Thomas and Pitts could be dead, victims of whatever had crippled the submersible.

"You and Nathan make sure you're careful getting the winch hooked up," Louis warned. "We have no idea what we're dealing with down there. It's going to be dangerous enough even if you both stay out of the water."

"Roger that," Brandon said and headed back into the rear compartment to get to work.

****

Chief Dixon looked over the battered hull of the X-29, appraising the damage that had been done to it. The submersible sat on where Louis' copter had deposited it on the wide, open expanse of the Alpha One platform's forward section. The X-29 had taken quite a beating. Long grooves were slashed into the armor of its hull. None of them were deep enough to have penetrated it, but they were more than a little disturbing. What kind of sea life had the strength to do something like this to the X-

29? Nothing that Dixon knew of that was for sure. His gaze shifted to the dents that also peppered the hull of the X-29. The strength behind those kinds of blows had to be enormous.

The X-29's forward window had been shattered and the submersible was flooded with salt water. A good portion of the water had leaked out of through the broken window during the flight to the station, but when they had opened its side door, water had still poured out it as if they had cracked open a fish tank. There was no sign of Pitts or Thomas. Both men were simply gone. Dixon's best guess was that whatever had shattered the forward window had dragged the two men out through it before Louis and the rescue team had arrived to collect the X-29.

As Dixon walked around the X-29 where it sat continuing to examine the damage, Cheryl hung back, watching him. Hank stood beside her, a loaded 12 gauge held ready in his hands. Despite the fact that Dixon had cleared the X-29 in regards to immediate threats, Hank remained on guard.

The only other member of the Alpha One Platform's crew present was Riggs, the platform's engineer and mechanic. His mouth continued to hang open as he took in the full scope of the damage the X-29 had suffered.

When Dixon was finished with his inspection, he approached where the others stood. "Cheryl, I know you don't want to hear this, but I think the platform needs to remain on high alert."

Before Cheryl could start to protest, he added, "Whatever did this, whatever those things were that we saw in the video stream from the X-29's final moments, they're still out there."

Cheryl gave a reluctant nod.

"You really think they're a threat to this platform, Chief?" Hank asked.

Dixon gestured at the shotgun in Hank's hands. "You wouldn't be carrying that if I didn't," he pointed out. "We don't know crap about those things. For all we know, they could be out there in the water right now, circling us."

"I thought you said they were squids," Riggs spoke up.

"No," Cheryl answered. "We said they looked like squids. They're not though. There's not a squid alive today that could do that kind of damage to the X-29."

"But we're not really talking about today, are we?" Dixon reminded her.

"Whatever these things might be, Chief Dixon, they're not what Thomas was after in the trench," Cheryl said firmly.

"I know," Dixon said, scowling. "Doesn't make me feel any better. In fact, it worries the holy hell out of me."

"I can tell you think these squid creatures and what Thomas was after are connected somehow, but I'm not sure that's a leap we can make without more evidence," Cheryl argued.

"I don't suppose it matters." Dixon sighed. "What does matter is how we're going deal with this mess. We have less than two days to pick up and then we're out of here. Two days can be a long time though. There's no reason to think those creatures won't come after this platform next."

"There's no reason to think that will either." Cheryl looked out at the water in the direction of the trench. "Most likely, they're territorial and were protecting their home. It's unlikely that they will leave the area surrounding the trench. We've been out here for nearly six months and haven't experienced a single encounter with them until now."

"Yeah, well, you said that whatever Thomas was after was, how did you put it, asleep. Why couldn't these things have been asleep too?" Dixon asked.

"And you believe the X-29's intrusion into the trench woke them up?" Cheryl shot back at him. "You're not an expert on sea life, Chief Dixon. Don't pretend to be one."

"I'm a guy who listens to his gut, ma'am, and right now, it's telling me we're in a world of trouble." Dixon looked to Hank for support. Hank was the only other security officer on the platform and the two of them had worked together for a long time. They had been through some scary, messed-up, and dangerous crap before but nothing like what they could be facing with the squids out there.

"I understand the need for caution, Chief Dixon," Cheryl said. "I really do. I think you're overreacting, however. As long as we don't send anyone else to the trench and keep out of the water, I just don't honestly see how those creatures could be a real threat to us."

"I hope you're right," Dixon told her. "We need to play this safe though, and that means Hank and I will be staying armed at all times. I want Gary and Rita armed as well. Wouldn't hurt to hand out weapons to Brandon and Nathan too. All of them can handle themselves and have at least some training."

"That's a lot of armed people, Dixon." Cheryl's voice was tense and Dixon knew he was on the edge of pushing her too far.

"We'll establish rotating watch up here," Dixon continued. "And whoever is on comm. duty inside will need to keep an eye out with the platform's sensors too."

Seeing Cheryl was on the verge of exploding at him, Dixon tried to head it off. "Look, ma'am, having a few people armed and exercising some caution isn't going to hurt anything. If I am wrong, doing that much doesn't cost us anything. It won't even look bad in your reports. If I am right though, that those things could be a threat to this platform, the things I am suggesting just might save all our lives."

"Fine," Cheryl consented. "I still think you're overreacting though. We'll have a briefing tonight so that everyone knows what's happening with this situation and how we're dealing with it."

"I think that's a fantastic idea, ma'am." Dixon smiled. "Hank can take the first watch alone since he's already in the 'know.' Gary and Rita can relieve him after the meeting."

****

The called briefing took place at shortly after 5 PM. The crew of the Alpha One Platform gathered in its mess hall. Brandon and Nathan kept to the rear of the large room with Louis. Cheryl and Dixon stood at its front. Riggs sat with Bailey, McCloud, and Rita, while Gary sat alone, nursing a steaming mug of coffee at a table near theirs. Only Hank and Peterson were absent. Someone had to remain on duty at the platform's comm. station and Peterson had volunteered for the job. He was already better informed about what was happening than most of the others.

Before Dixon and Cheryl could get started, Bailey called out, "Is it true then? Are Thomas and Pitts really dead?"

At her question, the others in the mess hall all fell silent, listening, and waiting to hear Dixon's response.

"We have to assume so," Dixon answered. "The X-29 was empty when Louis and the rescue team brought it home."

"There was no sign of them in the water," Louis chimed in to confirm what he was saying.

"What happened out there?" Bailey asked. "Thomas was so sure that he had found something truly special in that trench. Did he?"

"We don't know," Cheryl answered, taking the question herself. "You know as well as I do, Bailey, that the creatures we all just watched in the video Dixon played weren't what he was after."

Bailey was a marine biologist like Cheryl and Thomas. She and Thomas had grown to be close friends during their time together on the Alpha One Platform. Her eyes were red from tears at the news of Thomas' fate but those tears must have been shed earlier because right now she was as professional as ever. "I saw the creatures, Cheryl. I know that they weren't what he was after, but that doesn't mean he didn't find it. Something I don't get though is why you're so ready to dismiss these creatures as being unconnected to the lifeform that Thomas went into that trench after."

"Thomas showed you the data had on the thing in the trench, Bailey. I know he did. The lifeform he was hunting had to be enormous and ancient. Those things that attacked the X-29 don't appear to be either," Cheryl pointed out.

Bailey shook her head. "You have no evidence as to their age or where they came from. Did you ever stop to think that maybe they're this lifeform's offspring, or that maybe they're a part of how it defends itself while in its dormant state?"

Dixon saw Cheryl blink. It looked as if Bailey had brought up something Cheryl hadn't considered or didn't want to consider.

"Doctors!" Dixon cut in, overpowering the two of them with his booming voice that echoed in the mess hall. "There's no reason for us to be at each other's throats over this. What we need to be focusing on is how to keep this platform safe if those squid things are a threat."

"Tell him," Bailey suddenly demanded. "I know you saw it too."

"Saw what?" Dixon asked, confused.

"The tentacles on those things," Gary jumped into the conversation. Gary shot a glance at Bailey and said, "I saw them too."

"Great." Dixon clinched his fists at his sides trying to keep his temper under control. "Anyone want to clue me in?"

"They're not normal," Gary said. "They look to be the biological version of weapons, but even more than that, based on what little we can tell from the video, they have features that indicate they could be used as either arms or legs as needed."

"I don't understand," Dixon admitted. "What does that mean, blast it?"

It was Cheryl who answered. "It means they appear as if they could be used to walk on land or perhaps even climb with."

Cheryl's words hit him like a blow to the stomach and left his mind reeling. Dixon was silent for a moment while he processed them.

"But that's all just speculation," Cheryl blurted out. "The images on that video are badly distorted and appearance of something isn't definitive that it really does serve the purpose it appears to."

It was Riggs who spoke up next, addressing his question to Gary. "Are you saying those squid things could be amphibious? That's crazy, man. Who's ever heard of a squid that could live out of water?"

The sound of blaring alarm klaxons filled the mess drowning out Gary's reply. Dixon sprang into action, darting out of the mess. McCloud, Gary, Rita, Brandon, and Nathan followed after him.

****

Peterson stood looking out the window of the platform's control room, his eyes wide, and his mind reeling. There were squid-like monsters everywhere. The things had scaled the sides of the platform using their primary tentacles to haul their bodies up. Hank barely had any time to react. Their attack had come so quickly and unexpectedly, Hank apparently hadn't even known the things were scaling the sides of the platform until the first ones were already coming up. To his credit, Hank had stood his ground, pumping a round into the chamber of his shotgun. As one of the monsters approached him, Hank had blown the squid-thing back to whatever Hell it had been born in. The weapon's blast had virtually torn the soft body of the squid-thing apart in an explosion of black blood and gore. Peterson had detected the monsters in the waters around the platform but had made the mistake of assuming they couldn't actually get onto it. Guilt stung him as he watched Hank die. Another of the monsters scrambled across the platform's deck and slammed into Hank before he could ready his shotgun for a second shot. The monster held Hank to the deck with its lesser tentacles while its primary two stabbed into Hank over and over again. Blood flew from Hank's twitching body. Peterson knew the twitching had to be just from the shock Hank's body had been dealt as the first blow from the squid had plunged the spear-like tip of one of the creature's primary tentacles into and through Hank's skull. Peterson had managed to hold it together enough to slam a fist onto the controls that activated the platform's alarms, but now he was frozen in place, watching a tide of tentacle monsters swarm all over the platform's exterior surface.

The door to the control room burst open behind him. He turned to see Cheryl and Riggs enter.

"What's going on?" Cheryl snapped, moving to silence the platform's alarms.

Riggs joined at the window though, muttering, "Bloody hell."

"Where are the others?" Peterson stammered.

"Dixon took them to the armory, I think. They were heading out to see what the trouble was," Cheryl answered.

"They're as good as dead then," Riggs commented. "Ain't nothing going to survive those things swarming outside."

Cheryl finally took a look out the window. She took a step back from it at what she saw and turned to Peterson. "Get on the intercom, the radio, whatever it takes, and tell Dixon and the rest not to go outside."

"Too late for that," Peterson answered as he pointed at the platform's primary external door which had just opened. Dixon emerged from it leading the rest of the group that had gone with him. All of them appeared to be armed. A cacophony of gunfire and screams rang out as Dixon's group was met head on by the dozens upon dozens of squid creatures already aboard the platform. Dixon brought up his shotgun, firing directly into a mass of the squids that came at him. The shotgun thundered splattering the platform's deck with black gore. McCloud was by his side, his pistol barking as he fired shot after shot at the squids. Brandon and Nathan had spread out to the sides of the doorway the group had emerged from. Brandon was carrying a P-90. He hosed the squids with a stream of automatic fire that left several of the creatures flopping about on the deck. Nathan, like Dixon, carried a shotgun. He never got the chance to use it though. As Nathan raised the weapon, a squid that had attached itself to the platform's wall above the doorway dropped onto him. Nathan screamed as the monster's form covered the upper half of his body, its tentacles tearing at his flesh. Gary whirled in an attempt to help Nathan. He opened up at the monster on top of Nathan with the P-90 he carried. The rounds it spat tore through Nathan and the squid writhing about on him alike. Nathan and the squid toppled to the deck, red blood mixing with black. Rita slapped the barrel of Gary's weapon downwards but too late. Nathan was already dead.

"You idiot!" Rita cried at Gary. "What have you done?"

Before Gary could answer her, a tentacle shoved is way through her, bursting from the center of her chest in an explosion of blood. The tentacle lifted her from the deck and flung her into the wall beside the doorway. Gary stared at the squid that had just killed Rita in utter horror. He stumbled backwards away from it, bringing up the barrel of his P-90 level with its central mass. Gary squeezed the weapon's trigger. The squid seemed to know what was coming though. It flung itself upwards into the air. The burst of fire from Gary's weapon flew through the spot it had been a fraction of a second before. Gary's mouth opened in a scream as the squid landed on him. One of its primary tentacles wrapped itself around his right leg, jerking it, causing Gary to topple over even as its other primary tentacle slammed into and through his left shoulder. Gary thudded to the deck, struggling to free himself from the grasping secondary tentacles of the squid as they latched onto him. The last thing Gary saw was the squid's mouth coming towards his face then there was only a flash of red, his own blood flying, and then a cold, eternal blackness.

Dixon blew another squid to bits with a point blank blast from his shotgun and pumped a fresh round into its chamber. He knew that he and the others were dead unless they could get back inside the platform and close the door. Running towards the open doorway, he didn't see the squid that came at him from his right. It hit him with enough force to knock him from his feet and send him rolling across the deck.

Watching it all from the platform's control room, Riggs shook his head sadly as Cheryl turned to Peterson.

"Can that door be closed remotely?" Cheryl shouted.

"I ..." Peterson started but then seemed to get a hold of himself. "Yeah. Yeah, it can be."

"Do it!" Cheryl ordered him.

Bailey had entered the control room now too and had seen what was happening outside. "If you close that door, Peterson, you'll be killing Dixon and everyone that went out there with him," she warned.

"We don't have a choice," Cheryl snapped at her.

"There's always a choice," Bailey spat back at her.

"We don't have time for this," Riggs growled. "Close the fragging door, Peterson!"

Peterson nodded and dove into the chair of the system's control station. His fingers flew over the keyboard there. "It's done," he said, looking up and over at Cheryl.

Outside, Dixon was on his feet again. The squid that had hit him lay dead on the deck, most of its body reduced to black-smeared pulp. The round had been the last one in Dixon's shotgun, but it had been put to good use. Dixon ran back towards the doorway as he saw it was beginning to close itself.

"Everybody get back inside! Now!" he yelled.

Brandon, who was closest to the closing doorway and in the process of shoving a fresh mag into the P-90 he carried, ducked through the door. McCloud started after him only to come face to face with a hissing squid. The hook of one of the monster's primary tentacles swept upwards from the deck to embed itself in the tender flesh between McCloud's legs. McCloud screamed as the tentacle jerked back, taking his manhood and a good portion of his flesh with it.

"McCloud!" Dixon shouted as he watched the squid that had taken the man down slither on top of him. McCloud struggled beneath the mass of writhing tentacles that were wrapping themselves around his body. The squid's mouth found the side of McCloud's throat and ended him with a bite that sent geysers of hot red spraying over its grayish body.

"Sir!" Dixon heard Brandon shout at him as the door continued to close. "I can't stop it!"

Dixon saw the distance left between himself and the closing doorway and knew he would never make it through in time. Accepting his fate, he threw his empty shotgun aside, stopping in his tracks and drew the pistol holstered on his hip. If he was going to die, he was at least going to go down fighting.

The 9mm jerked in his hands as he held it in a two-handed grip and emptied the pistol's mag into a squid that came bounding across the deck towards him. Each round he fired tore through the squid's body. The squid shrieked in pain but kept coming. It hit him like a runaway truck, knocking the air from his lungs and taking him down under it. Other squids rushed to join it as it began to stab at him with its primary tentacles. Dixon howled as their spear-like tips pierced him. He kicked at the squid that had brought him down, trying to force it away from him. His heavy boot slammed into the creature's central body, but he barely jarred the thing. The squids were impossibly strong. Another of the squids that had gathered around him slipped a tentacle around his throat. It twisted tighter and tighter around Dixon there choking him and tearing away his skin. Blood flowed from beneath where the tentacle clutched him. Dixon dropped his empty pistol, raising both hands in an attempt to pry the tentacle loose from his neck. As he did so, another squid joined the struggle. One of its primary tentacles shot outwards to plunge into his chest. Dixon stared at the horrible appendage that had just rammed its way through his body as he went into shock. Then, suddenly, the world was spinning. The squids seemed to be getting farther and farther away from him. It took Dixon a moment to realize his head was no longer attached to the rest of him and was rolling across the deck. His vision narrowed as his brain began to die and the world in front of his eyes grew dark.

The doorway thudded closed in front of Brandon. No one else in the group that Dixon had led outside had survived. Brandon retreated several steps from the door as the squid creatures on its other side began to attack it. He heard the pounding of their tentacles as the monsters bashed them against the door in a frenzied madness trying to get inside and at him.

Brandon sprinted along the corridor, leaving the door behind him, as he ran for his life.

****

"The door is closed, ma'am," Peterson said.

"I can see that!" Cheryl snapped from where she stood at the control room's window. She had no delusion though that the door being sealed was going to keep the monsters out of the platform's interior. She had seen what the squids had done to the X-29's hull. Given time, the monsters would tear through the door, but they didn't need to. There were other means of getting inside the platform and she was standing beside one of them. She turned her gaze back outward across the platform's deck as her fears became reality. The glass of the window shattered in front of her. Shards of it flew into the control room as several tentacles broke through the bottom of the window. Cheryl screamed.

Riggs grabbed Cheryl from behind and dragged her away from the window. "We've got to get out of here!"

Bailey stood, mouth open in terror, staring at the squids that were pulling themselves up into the control. Riggs shoved her aside as he pushed Cheryl out of the control room. Glancing over his shoulder, he saw that Peterson was still at his station. Peterson was yelling out a distress message over the platform's long-range comm.

"This is research station Platform Alpha One! Mayday! I repeat, Mayday! We are under attack and require assistance!" Peterson cried.

"Come on, man!" Riggs shouted at Peterson as Bailey shook off her shock and ran out of the control room to join Cheryl in the corridor beyond it.

Peterson looked over at Riggs as if he was going to shout something back. His mouth opened but all that came out of it was a scream as one of the squids sprang through the window, a tentacle whipping outward in an arc. Its spear-like tip silenced Peterson's cry, reducing his throat to little more than a mess of shredded, jagged meat. Blood spurted from what remained of Peterson's throat as he raised his hands to press against the wound, vainly trying to stop the geysers of blood erupting from it.

Riggs threw himself out of the room without looking back. He knew Peterson was dead. There was no surviving a wound like that. "Shut the door!" he yelled at Cheryl and Bailey. Cheryl moved to the keypad beside it, typing in the code to lock the control room down. The door slide closed as a trio of tentacles lashed out at her. They were caught by it. The door crushed the tentacles, severing them. They flopped to the corridor floor, writhing there as Cheryl covered her mouth with her hand trying not to be sick.

"Incredible," Bailey muttered.

"There's nothing incredible about what's happening here," Riggs spat at her.

"We need to find somewhere safe," Cheryl said. "The windows aren't the only way in."

Riggs realized what she meant. There was an open pool in the depths of the platform that was used to launch the group's other submersible, a standard mini-sub designed for deep sea exploration and recon. "Frag," he shook his head, "she's right."

Thinking things over for a second, Riggs said, "The only place onboard with doors thick enough that they might hold against those things is engineering. If we can make it there, we might just be able to hold out until help comes."

"Good plan," Cheryl said, nodding. "Let's get moving."

"We need to hit the armory first," Riggs protested. "If those things do get into engineering ..."

"We'll need supplies too," Bailey pointed out. "Water shouldn't be an issue as long as the platform's power stays on, but who knows how long it will take for someone to respond to the message Peterson sent out."

If anyone even heard it, Riggs thought. His mind was having a hard time accepting that the three of them were the only members of the platform's staff and crew that were still alive. Then he realized why. "Hey!" Riggs looked over at Cheryl. "Where's Louis?"

Neither Cheryl nor Bailey answered him at first.

"I didn't see him with the others that went outside," Riggs said.

Cheryl shrugged. "Last I heard from him he was refueling the copter after the rescue team came in with the remains of the X-29."

"Does it matter?" Bailey protested. "We're in no position to help him. We'll be lucky if we can even make it to engineering and get it sealed up."

Riggs knew Bailey was right. Hating himself for giving up on Louis so easily, he gave a sharp nod. "Right then," he said. "Come on."

Riggs lead the way as the three of them sprinted down the corridor towards the platform's armory.

****

Louis had been inside the platform's helicopter when the attack began. The squids had come out of nowhere and their numbers seemed endless. The things were everywhere now. He had watched Hank die and then Dixon and the others after him, sitting paralyzed by fear in the copter's pilot seat. So far, the creatures hadn't noticed him. He knew they would, given time, but for the moment, he appeared to be safe. He thought about powering up the copter and taking off. It had a full tank. He could stay airborne for over eight hours with the copter's modified tanks, but eight hours seemed such a short time. From the looks of things outside the copter, the platform was done for. The squids had slaughtered Dixon and those who had come outside with him. The squids had torn through the door leading into the platform's interior within a matter of minutes of it being closed, and Louis knew very well that other ways inside too. If there was anywhere aboard the platform that would be safe, it would be either the armory or the engineering. Both had much heavier and denser doors than the rest throughout the platform. It was a good bet that anyone left alive would head for engineering though. It offered the larger space and running water. Louis also knew he could never make it there himself. As soon as he stepped out of the copter and the squids noticed him, they would swarm him and tear him to shreds.

Slumping down further in the copter's pilot seat, he listened to the hissing and screeching of the squid-like monsters as those that hadn't entered its interior wandered about its deck. Taking off appeared to be the only option left to him. He slowly reached up to start the copter's preflight routine. Seconds ticked away between each of his movements as he did his best to remain hidden from the squids. What should have taken only a few minutes to do stretch to over half of an hour. When he finished the last of the checks and saw that everything was green, he took a deep breath, steeling himself, and leaped up right into the pilot seat. He kicked the copter into gear. As its blades began to spin and the copter roared to life, every squid on the platform seemed to turn towards the copter. It would take about sixty seconds to get airborne. Louis could only pray the squids would give him that much time. None of the things were close to the helicopter. The closest of them still had a decent amount of distance to cover to get at it. The squids moved as one. They came swarming over the platform's deck towards the copter. Louis watched them coming and knew the copter wasn't going to be able to lift off before they reached it. The creatures were insanely fast. Their movements reminded him of the tripods in H.G. Wells' *War of the Worlds,* only on speed. He shifted more power through the copter's systems. It rose from its landing pad as the first of the squids reached it. One of the monsters launched itself through the air, springing onto the forward window in front of him.

"Frag!" Louis wailed but the copter was airborne now. He jerked it hard to port and away from the deck of Platform Alpha One. The squid on the window slid off of it, unable to find anything to hold on to. As it fell one, of its tentacles lashed out to hammer at the window. The blow sent hairline fractures across the glass but didn't shatter it completely. Louis was just happy to be able to see again. The copter rose in the sky as it cleared the side of the platform from his spur of the moment evasive maneuver. He wasn't out of trouble yet though. Several of the squids clung to the copter's skids and were even now pulling themselves up slither inside it through the open side door.

Though it was against regulations, Louis kept a .45 strapped to the underside of his pilot seat. He reached for the weapon and slid it out from underneath the seat. Turning to angle himself where he could fire into the copter's rear, Louis took aim at a squid. His hand was shaking. He forced it steady as he pulled the pistol's trigger. The pistol bucked in his grip as he fired. As strained as his nerves were, he nearly dropped it, but his shot flew straight and true. It blew a chunk of out of the squid's central mass. The thing screeched and lost its hold on the side of the copter. It vanished from sight as it fell downward into the waters of the ocean below. A second squid took its place almost as quickly as it had fallen. Louis had counted four of the things in total that had made it onto the copter's skids. He could see the third squid behind the second waiting for its turn to slide through the copter's side door. There was no sign of the fourth and that worried him.

Louis acted faster against the second squid. He didn't aim so much as just point the pistol's barrel in the creature's general direction and let loose. He emptied half the pistol's mag. into the squid. The creature gave a high -pitched, pained wail that stung his ears as the rounds hammered into its central mass. Louis didn't know crap about the weak points of the squids' bodies, but apparently, he had gotten lucky and hit something vital. The squid slumped forward to collapse onto the floor of the copter's rear. It laid there, a pool of black blood growing around it, as the third squid entered the copter. Louis jerked his head around as the copter's window shattered and shards of glass rained over him. The fourth squid must have somehow crawled along the underside of the copter to scale up its front. The already fractured window had stood no chance against the thing. The first blow from its tentacles had smashed it open. Several of the shards of glass had struck Louis with enough force to pierce his skin. He grunted at the pain, swinging his pistol around at the squid that was nearly on top of him. Louis squirmed in the copter's pilot seat, dodging tentacles that lashed out at him, as he emptied the remainder of the pistol's magazine into the squid, point blank. Black blood splashed over his face and got into his mouth. It tasted like a mix of vinegar and motor oil. Louis spat it out even as the squid was knocked from the front of the copter and fell out of his sight. The copter had started to spin out of control. Louis grabbed the flight stick and tried to right it. He had forgotten about the last squid in the copter's rear until one of its tentacles burst through both his seat and his body. He looked down at the spear-like tip of the tentacle that impaled his body, blood rushing up his throat to leak from the sides of his mouth. Louis tried to scream as the squid ripped the tentacle out of his body and moved around the pilot seat to come at him from his side. Alarms were blaring as the copter continued to spin out of control. Louis tried to reach of the flight stick again as he had lost his hold on it when the squid's tentacle had plunged through him but found he couldn't move his arms. He figured the tentacle must have severed his spine as it had impaled him. The squid gave a hiss and lunged at him, its mouth coming at his face.

Seconds later, the helicopter struck the surface of the ocean like a fist punching through a pane of glass.

****

Captain John Weaver sat behind the desk in his office replaying the distress call for the fifth time.

"This is research station Platform Alpha One! Mayday! I repeat, Mayday! We are under attack and require assistance!" the voice yelled. He was sure the call was real. Nobody short of a professional act could fake the degree of panic and utter terror in the man's voice who had made the call. There was nothing more to the call though. No indication of who was attacking the platform or anything else in regards to whatever was happening there.

Weaver had his XO, Ennis, pull everything there was available on Platform Alpha One. It turned out that the platform was a corporate-owned research facility dedicated to the study of marine biology and deep sea exploration. The facility was a small but high tech one. Such a platform was an unlikely target for all but the most desperate of pirates. Weaver figured a terrorist attack on the platform was a much more likely assumption but even that didn't make much sense. Unless Alpha Platform One was conducting unauthorized experiments in biological weapons or the like, there was no reason that came to mind that would make it a target for terrorists either. Why waste time and money on hitting such a secluded and relatively unknown target if you were a terrorist wanting to make a statement?

Rubbing at his cheeks in frustration, Weaver leaned back in his chair. His ship, the *USS Braxton*, was on routine training maneuvers and most of his crew was made up of newbies still getting a feel for the ship and how he ran it. Though the ship was fully armed and ready for action itself, his crew wasn't.

Weaver sighed. The *Braxton* was the only ship close enough to be able to respond in kind of reasonable amount of time though and that left him little choice. If he didn't answer the platform's distress call, whatever happened there was on him and he knew it.

A knock sounded on his office door. He looked up to see Ennis standing in the open doorway staring at him.

"Come on in, Ennis." Captain Weaver motioned his XO towards one of the chairs in front of his desk. "And close the door behind you if you would."

"Yes, sir," Ennis answered, closing the door and taking a seat in front of his desk. "I am sorry to bother you, sir, but…"

"Let me guess," Captain Weaver said, frowning, "the whole ship already knows about the distress call that's come in and they're wondering what we are going to do about it?"

Ennis chuckled. "That's it exactly, sir."

Captain Weaver shrugged, still frowning. "There is nothing we can do but respond to it."

"I sort of figured that, sir," Ennis admitted.

"Get us on a course to the platform at maximum military speed," Captain Weaver ordered. "Tell Sergeant Dawson to have his men ready to board the platform. Make sure that Dawson understands that we have no idea what we'll be heading into."

"Yes, sir." Ennis nodded. "Dawson has got a lot of experience in these situations. I am sure he'll take every precaution."

"Go ahead and sound action stations as we get underway for the platform," Weaver added. "I don't think we'll run into anything this ship can't handle, but it's always better to be prepared than not."

"Agreed," Ennis said. "I still haven't been able to get any current satellite photos of the platform. A storm rolled into the area not long after we received the distress call from it. The cloud cover is playing havoc with—"

"Doesn't matter." Captain Weaver waved a dismissive hand at his XO. "We're going in one way or another. It's our job, Ennis."

"The storm is likely to mess with our own comm. systems too, sir," Ennis protested in spite of what he had said.

Captain Weaver ignored him, opening the drawer of his desk to produce a bottle of vodka and two shot glasses. He poured both glasses full and offered one to Ennis.

"Have you had time to read over the information I was able to dig up about the platform and its purpose, sir?" Ennis asked as he took the glass Captain Weaver handed him.

Captain Weaver nodded. "Everything points to it just being another research facility and a legit one at that."

Ennis downed his glass in a single swallow and shook his head. "Strong stuff."

"The best a captain's salary can buy anyway." Captain Weaver grinned and slammed the contents of his own glass down his throat.

"You're right about Platform Alpha One being legit, sir," Ennis said, settling back to business. "That's a good thing. At first, I thought it might be a cover for something more not so on the up and up."

"Bioweapons." Captain Weaver nodded. "I thought about that too. Thank God it honestly doesn't appear to be a home to anything like that."

"Which really begs the question…" Ennis went on.

"Of who would attack it," Captain Weaver finished for him and sat his empty glass on his desk beside the bottle of vodka. "I guess we'll be finding out soon enough."

****

Specialist Warren Hawks checked the magazine one final time before slamming it home in his rifle. His expression was grim as he looked over at Larson. Larson was grinning like a feral cat that had just discovered a rat trapped in the room with it.

"Don't look so bent out of shape, Hawks," Larson said, smirking. "I thought this trip was going to be boring as Hades. Now at least we're going to get see some action."

The two of them were the senior members of the small rescue-and-boarding party that was going to be heading over to the platform the distress call had come in from when the *Braxton* reached it. They were still over an hour out, but Larson was already ready to go. Being cooped up on the ship hadn't been kind to Larson. He was fresh out of the Sand Box and his "strings were vibrating."

Hawks set his rifle aside and lit up a cigarette. He inhaled, long and deep, before letting the smoke flow slowly out of his lungs then answered, "Larson, take a look around you, buddy. These kids ain't ready for the type of action you're itching for."

Larson snorted. "They have to learn someday and today's as good a day as any."

"You need to relax, man," Hawks told him. "We've got no idea what we're heading into."

Hawks' statement seemed contradictory it was but a truth he knew from experience that keeping a level head in the field was the best thing one could do if they wanted to stay alive.

Robbie, one of the new squad members, approached them. He saluted Larson. "Sir!"

"At ease." Larson nodded.

"Thank you, sir." Robbie smiled. "I was wondering if I could join you?"

"It's a free country." Larson shrugged.

"Actually, we're not in a country at all," Hawks corrected him. "These are international waters."

Larson glared at him. "Always got to be smart, don't ya?"

Hawks flashed a wry grin as Robbie took a seat on a crate near the ones they sat on.

"This your first op, kid?" Larson asked.

"Yes, sir," Robbie replied, nodding nervously.

"Drop the sir crap," Larson told Robbie. "We're off the clock right now."

Robbie shifted uncomfortably on the crate he had taken a seat on. "Do you really think it was terrorists that hit the platform, uh, Mr. Larson?"

Hawks nearly doubled over laughing. "Just call him Larson, kid. That's his name."

Robbie's cheeks flushed red, but he kept his eyes fixed on Larson, waiting for an answer.

"How in the devil would I know?" Larson growled. "Do I look psychic to you?"

"I just thought…" Robbie started.

"Having seen some action and earning some rank doesn't make you all-knowing, kid," Hawks chimed in. "We don't know anything more than you guys do."

Robbie was clearly disappointed by his answer.

"We'll be finding out what we're up against soon enough," Hawks said.

"And we'll be ready for it too," Larson added. "Oorah!"

"Aren't you going to inspect our gear?" Robbie asked.

"Great," Larson shook his head, "first, this kid thinks I'm psychic, and now, he thinks I'm his babysitter."

"Don't let Larson get to you," Hawks told Robbie. "He's in a mood today. Just bring along anything you think you'll need that won't slow you down and don't skimp on the ammo. If things go all pear-shaped and we get stuck on that platform, you'll be grateful to have it. Pass that on to the others too."

"Will do," Robbie said, getting to his feet. He headed over to join the other three green members of the squad.

Hawks watched the kid go. "Think you were a bit rough on him?"

"Me? Never," Larson chuckled. "Whoever hit that platform though, they're likely to tear him a new one when we get there."

****

Captain Weaver sat in his command chair on the bridge of the *USS Braxton*. He drummed his fingers on the arm of the chair as the battleship sped over the waves in route to the Platform Alpha One facility.

"Sir, we're coming up on the platform now," Watkins, the helmsman, informed him.

Ennis, the ship's XO, stood beside Weaver's command chair, frowning.

"We've got visual contact, Captain," the sonar/comm tech on duty, Lancaster, reported.

"Put it on screen," Weaver ordered.

An image of the platform filled the tactical display.

"What in the devil are those things?" Ennis muttered, losing his professional composure as the image appeared.

The deck and sides of the platform were alive with creatures that moved and slithered about over them. There were hundreds of the creatures. Each was close to the size of a man or slightly larger. The whole scene was something like out of a deranged nightmare.

"Are those squids?" Watkins asked.

"Never seen a squid that could climb like those things are before," Lancaster commented. "I mean look at them. They're actually climbing and hanging onto the edges of the platform."

"God help us," Captain Weaver heard Ennis say from beside him.

"There are hundreds of them," Lancaster reported. "I'm picking up more of them in the water surrounding the platform too."

Captain Weaver grunted. "I guess we know what attacked the platform now."

"Where did those things come from?" Watkins asked no one in particular.

"Lancaster, hail the platform," Captain Weaver ordered, not taking his eyes off the image of the squid-like monsters swarming over it.

"Hailing the platform now, sir," Lancaster said. "No reply, sir," he added after a few seconds ticked by.

Captain Weaver glanced over at Ennis. The XO looked pale. There was nothing in the book about dealing with a situation like this. Sending the strike team over to the platform would likely be suicide for the marines that were prepped and ready to go. There could very well be people left alive inside the platform, however, and something had to be done to try to help them.

"Options?" Captain Weaver asked.

"We're gonna need to clear that deck if we do send a strike team over," Ennis said.

Captain Weaver glared at the XO for stating the obvious.

"I think controlled bursts from the *Braxton*'s CIWS would be the fastest means of doing so," Ennis told him.

Captain Weaver nodded. "Assuming the platform itself and can take that sort of barrage and remain intact."

"According to the data we have on the platform," Lancaster chimed in, "it's pretty tough. If we take our time and we're careful, the CIWS should be able to clear the deck without too much damage to the platform's structure."

"Agreed." Ennis nodded.

"Keep the strike team on standby until we do so," Captain Weaver ordered. "And let's be about it then."

"It'll take me a few minutes to work things out with the CIWS and get it configured for what we're doing," Ennis said.

"I'm on it," Smith, the *Braxton*'s weapons officer, spoke up.

"Understood," Captain Weaver replied.

As Ennis and Smith went about their work, Captain Weaver continued to watch the creatures swarming over Platform Alpha One. What were they? Where did they come from? There was so much that he didn't know that he needed to know, and the only people who might have those answers, if they were still alive, were the platform's crew. There was no sign of anyone on the platform. Captain Weaver had to assume that the creatures on its deck and sides were hostile and had driven any surviving members of the platform's crew into the interior of its structure. The distress call the *Braxton* had received made it clear that the platform had been attacked and that attack had to have come from these creatures that now moved about the platform as if it were their own. Captain Weaver didn't like the idea of killing the creatures, all life mattered, but there was no other choice.

"Captain!" Lancaster called to him. "The contacts in the water are beginning to close on the *Braxton.*"

"More of those things like on the platform?" Captain Weaver asked.

"Yes, sir," Lancaster confirmed.

"Ennis?" Captain Weaver demanded.

"We've got the CIWS reconfigured, sir," Ennis barked.

"Then take those things closing and send them back to whatever Hell they crawled out of," Captain Weaver ordered.

"Yes, sir!" Smith shouted.

The *Braxton*'s CIWS rotated on its base, its barrels turning downward. The ship actually had two CIWS units, both prototype systems, that could target close-in surface contacts and not just airborne threats. The port CIWS roared to life. Its barrels thundered pumping a three thousand round a minute blast of fire into the water at the approaching creatures. The water above where the creatures were located splashed upwards towards the heavens as the rounds tore through its surface. The water churned beneath the fury of the barrage and grew black.

After a few seconds, the CIWS shutdown, falling silent.

"The remaining CBDR contacts have broken off and changed course, sir," Lancaster reported. "That hit them pretty hard. Based on the data coming in from the sonar, I'd say we halved their number at least."

"Good," Captain Weaver commented. "Smith?"

"Targeting the creatures on the platform now, sir," Smith answered.

"Short controlled bursts," Ennis reminded the weapons officer.

"Yes, sir," Smith responded from his seat at the weapons station.

The CIWS came to life again. It rotated on its base to target the platform. Captain Weaver held his breath as he watched the CIWS open fire at the platform. Using it in such a way was a gamble. There was no certainty that its fire wouldn't penetrate the platform's hull to the point of endangering anyone left inside its interior. The CIWS thundered again. It spat short burst after short burst at the creatures covering the platform's exterior surface. Captain Weaver watched the squid-like creatures struck by its fire being torn apart. Many of the squid-like things were nearly vaporized by the high-velocity rounds that ripped through their ranks. Black blood flew everywhere to the point that a black mist formed over the platform's primary deck and hung in the air like fog.

Several minutes later, the grizzly work was done. The platform hadn't been completely cleared, but the bulk of the squids aboard it had been utterly decimated. The CIWS fell silent again.

"That's it, sir," Smith spoke up. "Any more and the odds are of overly damaging the platform become too great."

Captain Weaver nodded. "Still no response to our hails?" he asked Lancaster.

"None, sir," Lancaster answered.

"Alright then," Captain Weaver said with a sigh. "Make Larson aware of the situation and get the strike team deployed."

"Sir…" Ennis started, but Captain Weaver stopped him.

"I am well aware that the boats will be open to attack on their trip over. We'll do what we can to cover them," Captain Weaver said.

****

The two small boats hit the water. Larson was the CO of the first boat, Hawks was over the second. Both boats sped across the waves towards Platform Alpha One. Each boat contained a squad of three counting its CO. Hawks was glad Robbie was on his boat. He had taken a liking to the kid and promised himself to look out for him. The third member of his squad was a tall, lanky trooper named Chuck. All three of them kept their eyes on the water and weapons ready. They had seen the things crawling on and over the platform they were headed for. The creatures creeped out Hawks more than he would ever admit. Things like these creatures, to him, shouldn't exist in the real world. Squids didn't walk around outside of the water much less climb the walls of structures like the platform. None of what was happening made sense. It was like stepping into a horror film.

"Movement to port!" Robbie shouted.

Chuck was manning the stick so that left Robbie and himself to make sure nothing got onto the boat with the three of them. Hawks raised his rifle but couldn't see anything. Robbie was a newbie and likely easily spooked, but Hawks didn't doubt the kid had seen something.

Hawks flinched and Robbie screamed as the *Braxton*'s CIWS swept the water not far from their boat with a barrage of fire.

"Hold it together, kid," Hawks cautioned him.

Robbie looked at him with wide eyes.

"We'll make it," Hawks assured him.

Larson's boat was close to the platform now. Larson was standing up in the boat, his rifle blazing away at something in the water near it. Hawks watched as the boat came alongside the platform and another member of Larson's squad fired a grappling hook up onto the side of the platform. It caught and held from the look of things. Larson was the last to abandon the boat. He kept firing into the water as the other two members of his squad climbed up it. Only when they were well out of reach of whatever was in the water did Larson stop shooting, shoulder his weapon by its strap, and start up the rope himself.

As Chuck steered their boat up the platform, he shouted, "Look out!"

Hawks turned his gaze upwards to see one of the squid creatures moving impossibly fast across the side of the platform above them towards their position. The thing moved like some sort of crazy spider. Robbie was just staring at the thing, watching it in terror. The newbie had gone pale. Hawks jerked up his rifle, taking aim at the creature. It gave a high-pitched screech as it leaped from the side of the platform. Hawks met it with a fully automatic stream of fire from his rifle. The rounds slashed through the thing's body. Black blood sprayed from its wounds as the impact of the bullets knocked it off its intended course and sent it spiraling to splash into the water beside the boat.

"Get the fragging grapple set!" Hawks ordered Robbie, slapping him on the shoulder. The *Braxton*'s CIWS was pouring rounds into the water behind the boat. Hawks could see dozens more squid creatures in the water there. The CIWS was making short work of most of them, but some were getting past its field of fire.

Robbie fired the grappling hook up onto the platform and checked to make sure it was well in place.

"What are you waiting for?" Hawks demanded. "Get moving!"

As Robbie started up the rope, Hawks clicked his weapon over to burst fire instead of full-auto mode. He aimed at one squid creature in the water after another, picking off the closest ones first and working his way outward with his shots.

Chuck went up the rope next. Only when the tall, lanky newbie was well up the rope after Robbie did Hawks turn to climb the rope himself. A squid he hadn't seen emerged from the waves nearly tipping the boat over as it hurled itself onto it. One of the thing's tentacles made a grab for him. It caught his lower left leg. Hawks grunted against the pain as he felt the tiny hooks that lined the underside of the tentacle tearing at his flesh through the cloth of his pants. The thing was incredibly strong. He couldn't jerk his leg free of its hold. Keeping a grip on the rope with one hand, Hawks swung himself sideways on the rope where he could angle the barrel of his rifle downward at the squid to get a better shot at it. He squeezed the rifle's trigger and put a three-round burst of fire into the squid creature's central mass. It shrieked as the bullets shredded its flesh where they struck. The thing's tentacle withdrew from his leg as Hawks fired a second burst into the creature to make sure it wouldn't be grabbing him again. The squid creature's body slumped over in the boat and lay there unmoving as Hawks slung his weapon onto his shoulder, taking hold of the rope with both hands, and started climbing as fast as he could.

He could hear gunfire above him. The others had already reached the main deck of the platform and engaged the squid creatures there. Hawks, breathing hard and pressing his body to its limits, made it to the top of the rope and pulled himself onto the platform's deck. Larson had the others in a semi-circle formation firing into the ranks of the dozens of squid creatures that came at them from all sides. The things were likely the last of their kind left on the platform's exterior, but that didn't mean they were going down without a fight. Hawks raised his rifle and joined the battle. He emptied the last few rounds in his rifle's magazine, blowing one of the squid creatures to bits as it charged at him. Black blood splattered over him. He flinched at the cold, slimy feel of it on his skin.

"Hold the line!" Larson shouted.

The others were doing their best to do just that. Hyatt, one of Larson's squad members, lobbed a grenade into the oncoming mass of squids.

"Fire in the hole!" Hyatt shouted before the grenade detonated. Its blast blossomed on the platform's deck, wiping out a good portion of the remaining squid creatures.

Dillon, the other member of Larson's squad, didn't notice the squid coming at him from his right. It plowed into him, knocking him from his feet. The spear-like tip of one of its primary tentacles slashed him open from his stomach to the bottom of his neck. Purple intestinal strands, slicked with red, bulged out of the wound, as the squid creature finished Dillon with a second swipe of its tentacle that took his head from his shoulders and sent it rolling across the deck.

Despite their losses, the squid creatures continued to press their attack. There were only a handful for them left now, and Hawks was eager to see the last of them dead. He ejected his rifle's spent magazine and slapped a fresh one into it, clicking the rifle back to full auto. Leveling the barrel of his weapon at the last of the squid creatures, he emptied the entire new magazine into them. The stream of bullets sent the squid creatures sprawling and flopping about the deck.

The battle came to an end as quickly as it had begun. Dillon had been their only causality and they were lucky in that regard. Things could have easily been much, much worse.

Hawks and the others held their position waiting to see if any more squid creatures that hadn't shown themselves in the initial onslaught were lurking about. There didn't appear to be any.

"On me," Larson ordered and started across the deck. The platform's main entrance door had been smashed inward, an impressive feat given that it was metal and designed to resist everything nature could hurl at it. Hawks couldn't help but think that there didn't seem to be anything natural about the monsters they were up against.

Hawks could see that the platform still had power. The corridor lights beyond the broken entrance door were on.

"Hawks, take point," Larson ordered. "Everybody keep sharp. Those things could be anywhere."

Hawks led the others into the corridor. As they entered the doorway, Robbie said, "Hold up."

"What?" Larson demanded.

"That control panel for the door," Robbie told him. "I think can access the central system of the platform from it."

Hawks saw Larson give him a questioning glance. "Let him do it. If he can pull the layout of this place…"

"Get to it then," Larson ordered Robbie. "The rest of you, take up defensive positions."

Chuck and Hawks moved to cover the corridor to the right while Larson and Hyatt covered the left. The corridor was disturbing quiet compared to the battle they had just lived through. The quiet set Hawks' nerves on edge.

Robbie popped the cover from the panel and dug his equipment out of his pack, settling into his work.

"You really think there's any still alive here?" Chuck whispered.

Hawks shrugged. "It's our job to find out."

The seconds ticked by like hours and the minutes like days. Finally, Robbie disconnected his tablet from the panel, grinning like a fiend. "I got everything we need and then some," Robbie told them.

Larson raised an eyebrow.

"I downloaded the layout of the platform and was even able to tie some system controls to my tablet. If we run into a locked-down door, I should be able to open it without having to interface again … as long as the power stays on anyway," Robbie added as an afterthought.

"Which way then?" Larson asked.

"The most logical places for anyone still alive to hole up are the platform's armory or its engineering section," Robbie said.

"This place has an armory?" Chuck shook his head in disbelief. "What the frag, man?"

"I say we try engineering first," Robbie finally answered Larson's question. "It's not only the larger of the two, but it would have facilities inside it."

"Facilities?" Chuck asked.

"He means places to relieve yourself and sinks," Hawks laughed. "What? Did you grow up in a barn?"

"Yeah, actually I did," Chuck said with a frown. "Got a problem with that, sir?"

"At ease, Chuck," Larson warned. "Robbie, let Hawks get a look at the schematics on your screen before we move out. I still want him on point."

Of course you do, Hawks thought. He couldn't really blame Larson for it though. Only the two of them had any real experience under their belts, and one of the newbies getting trigger happy or spooked and blowing away a survivor would be bad for them all.

The group got moving again. The closest route to the engineering section was to the right. According to the data Robbie downloaded, the corridor they were already in would take them straight to a lift that led down to the level engineering was located on.

They were halfway to the lift when Hawks heard something from a corridor that led off from the one they were in. He stopped, holding up a hand to tell the others behind him to as well. Hawks carefully leaned around the corner of the side corridor to steal a glance into it. At first, he didn't see anything then the squid creature on its ceiling moved. The thing hung upside like a bat, its tentacles somehow holding it tight to the corridor's ceiling. Its primary tentacles were coiled up and ready to strike at anything that came near it. Hawks didn't dare speak, even in a whisper, to let the others know it was there. Instead, he ever so slowly raised his rifle and took aim at the squid creature. If it saw him, it gave no indication of it. Hawks took a deep breath and said a prayer that the squid creature was the only one close by then squeezed his rifle's trigger. It chattered, spent round casings flying from its side to clatter to the corridor floor. Hawks put two three-round bursts into the squid's central mass, splattering its guts into the air. The creature's body fell from the ceiling to thud onto the corridor floor.

Hawks darted around the corner into the side corridor, his rifle ready, looking for any more squid creatures lying in wait there. There weren't any at least that he could see. He motioned for the others to continue along the corridor that led to the lift as he hung back to cover the side corridor. When the others were passed, he joined them bringing up the rear. Larson had taken over point.

As the lift came into view, it was clear it had been attacked. Though the interior of the lift looked fine, there was human blood smearing its walls and its battered doors lay ripped off on the floor in front of it. Larson waited for Hawks to move around the others and join him at the front of the group. Robbie stood with them his tablet in his hand.

"Robbie?" Larson asked.

"The lift is functional from what I can tell," Robbie answered. "Its systems show green."

"Somebody died here," Hawks commented.

"Makes you wonder where the body is then," Larson said.

"Maybe those things ate it," Chuck spoke up from behind them.

Hawks frowned stepping into the lift. "There may be more truth to that than you think."

He knelt and picked up a piece of a bone from the floor that couldn't be seen from outside the lift. He'd only noticed when he entered. Hawks held it up for the others to see.

"God have mercy," Hyatt muttered.

"God didn't have anything to do with what's happened here," Larson growled.

"We need to keep moving," Hawks urged Larson.

Larson nodded, motioning the others into the lift. The group filed into it. Larson knew the lift wouldn't move with its doors gone. "Robbie, can you…?"

"Override the safety protocols of this thing and get it going? Yeah, I can. Give me a sec," Robbie answered.

Robbie worked on his tablet for about a minute and then looked back up at Larson, grinning. "Here we go, sir."

The lift lurched as it started moving. It descended in its shaft, carrying the group to the level of the platform where the engineering section was located.

"Be ready," Larson warned the others. With the doors of the lift gone, they'd be completely open to anything that might be waiting on them when it reached its destination. Hawks removed the magazine from his rifle and traded it for a new one.

The lift stopped. The corridor outside of it appeared to be empty. The lights along its ceiling were mostly out though and the few that remained were flickering on and off.

"No issue with the power, sir," Robbie whispered to Larson. "This is actual damage to the lights here."

Larson nodded and gestured at Hawks. Hawks slowly advanced out of the lift. He looked up and down the corridor. There were shadows everywhere. As he continued along the corridor, Hyatt followed him. The big man didn't carry the standard issue rifle that Hawks and the others did. Instead, he carried an automatic shotgun. He'd switched out weapons during the ride on the lift. His rifle now hung from his back by its strap. Hawks was grateful to see Hyatt breaking out the heavier firepower. In such close quarters, the shotgun would be devastating to any squids that they encountered.

Nothing came at them. Hawks and Hyatt paused waiting on the others to catch up. "Which way?" Hawks asked.

Robbie pointed straight ahead of them. "That big door right up there," Robbie told them. "It leads into the engineering section."

The group approached the door and took up defensive positions around it, the barrels of their weapons aimed at the corridor behind them.

Hawks examined the doors with Larson. The heavy door had clearly been attacked by the squids. There was some impressive and scary damage to it. It had held though. The squid creatures hadn't been able to rip it down or break through it. It gave Hawks hope that someone might still be alive on its other side.

"Robbie," Larson urged the young specialist.

"Working on it, sir," Robbie said without looking up from the screen of his tablet.

Hawks heard something inside the wall next to the door click into place. The heavy door began to slide open inside its frame. It moved slowly as if something were wrong with the motor that made it function. Hawks moved to peer into the engineering section before the door was fully open. Only the grace of God and his instincts saved his life as a gun thundered from behind the door and a bullet pinged against the metal of the door's edge where his face had been a moment before as he jerked his head back.

"Don't shoot!" Hawks screamed at whoever was inside. "We're human!"

Hawks heard two people behind the door start yelling at each other, but he couldn't make out what they were saying. The door finally fully opened to reveal two women and a man standing several yards away from it. The taller woman clutched a still-smoking rifle aimed at the doorway. At the sight of him and the other soldiers outside the door, she lowered it, looking terrified and relieved at once.

"See? I told you help would come!" the shorter woman at her side shouted.

The man moved forward to rush Hawks and others the rest of the way into the engineering section. "Come on," he urged them. "We need to get this door closed again before those things out there show up!"

None of the soldiers argued with him, not even Larson. As soon as they were all inside, the man activated the door again and it slid closed behind them.

"My name is Riggs," the man told them. "That lady there holding the gun is Cheryl. She's in charge here."

"Sorry about taking a shot at you," Cheryl said weakly. "I thought those things had finally found a way in here."

"No harm done," Hawks lied. His nerves were wound up tight from the bullet hitting so close to him. "Just make sure you know what you're shooting at next time before you squeeze that thing's trigger." He gestured at the rifle she held.

Larson eyed the other woman. "And who are you?"

"My name is Dr. Heather Bailey. I was one of the platform's scientific staff," the woman answered.

"We're all that's left," Riggs said before Larson could ask. "Those things got all the others."

"Yeah, exactly what are those things?" Hawks asked.

"We don't know, not really," Bailey answered.

"Some of our crew was exploring a vast trench on the ocean floor when their submersible was attacked by the creatures. We know they came from that trench, but as to what they are... evolutionary throwbacks? Mutations? Really it's anybody's guess at this point," Cheryl said.

"Why was any of your crew even in the trench?" Chuck blurted out.

Larson and Hawks both glared at him for the idiotic question.

"It was their job," Riggs said firmly. "That's why this platform exists."

"To be more specific," Bailey cut in, "they were investigating something we picked up on our equipment. We had reason to believe that there was a lifeform in the trench. Something that mankind had never encountered before."

"The kind of discovery careers are made by," Hawks commented.

Bailey nodded, not trying to deny it. "Yes. Only we didn't have a clue that those things were down there. All our data pointed to a single, massive lifeform."

Larson raised an eyebrow. "And what happened to the lifeform you were searching for?"

Bailey shrugged. "As far as we know, the submersible was attacked before it was discovered."

"So whatever you first picked up could be out there too? I mean in addition to these ... whatever they are, squid creatures," Hawks pressed her.

"No question about it," Bailey confirmed. "Whatever it is, it's still there. Whether it's awake or not, that we have no means of knowing."

"Awake?" Larson frowned.

"We suspect that the massive lifeform is or must have been in some kind of dormant state, a type of hibernation if you will," Bailey explained.

"You guys just woke it up," Chuck growled. "And those things out there too."

Bailey looked as if she had just had an epiphany, "Yes!" she exclaimed, turning to Cheryl and Riggs "That's it. What if the squid creatures are the protectors of whatever the massive lifeform down there in the depths is? They have to be connected to it in some way and this man's assertion makes sense."

"Could be," Cheryl agreed. "Perhaps they were dormant too, but when the X-29 got to close to them in the trench, something about it woke them up and they sprang to the defense of the massive lifeform like white blood cells protecting a human body."

"Then that means this big thing down there that you were after, it's awake now too?" Larson asked.

Bailey shook her head. "Not necessarily."

"We better hope not." Larson raised his rifle. "These squid things are enough to deal with on their own. Any idea how many of them there might be?"

Neither Bailey nor Cheryl had an answer to his question.

"Uh huh," Larson said, scowling. "That figures. Well, I think the first thing we need to do is get the frag out of here and back onboard the *Braxton*."

"The *Braxton*?" Riggs asked. "That's your ship?"

Hawks nodded. "She's a battleship. We were on maneuvers when your distress call came in. Thankfully for you, Captain Weaver decided to respond to it."

Bailey looked like she wanted to ask what he meant by that last bit. Civilians often didn't get that sometimes the military had bigger things to deal with than playing search and rescue. Cheryl put a hand on the shorter woman's shoulder though, stopping her. Hawks could see that Cheryl knew exactly what he had meant.

"It's not going to be easy getting out of here," Riggs warned. "Those things are everywhere inside the platform. We barely made it here and got the doors sealed when everything started."

"Riggs, these men are professionals," Cheryl told him. "Clearly, they fought their way in and they can fight their way out too."

"Thanks for the vote of confidence, lady," Larson snorted. "We are professionals, but that don't mean it's going to be easy. We lost a man on the way in and that was without having all of you to watch out for."

"What Larson is trying to say is that we are going to need all of you to do exactly as you are told, no hesitation or arguing if you want to stay alive," Hawks said, doing his best take some of the demoralizing edge off Larson's way of putting things.

Larson extended his hand towards Cheryl, reaching for the shotgun she held. "Hand it over, lady," he ordered her. "I don't want to get shot in the back while I am trying to save your sorry butts."

Cheryl stared at him as if he were stark raving mad.

"She's keeping her weapon, sir." Riggs stepped over to the two of them. "And in fact, I want one too."

Larson looked like he was about to lose his cool. Hawks knew Larson didn't like being told what to do, despite it being a part of his job. He was used to be in complete command in the field at least of his own squad. Hawks moved to Larson's side. "Let her keep the gun. I'll watch out for her."

Larson shot him a sideways glance. "That lady almost blew your head off, buddy. You're crazy, you know that right?"

"Which means she won't be so quick to make that mistake again, right?" Hawks looked over at Cheryl.

"Right," she said, picking up on the fact that Hawks wanted her to agree with him and it was true. The incident with him had put the fear of God into her.

"See?" Hawks argued. "She'll be just fine."

"Fine," Larson grumbled. "She's your problem, Hawks. If she shoots you from behind, don't come crying to me."

"And what about me?" Riggs demanded.

Larson drew his sidearm, flipping it over in his hand, to offer it to Riggs.

"Thanks," Riggs said, accepting the weapon and readying it like a pro.

"Now if we're done here ..." Larson gestured towards the door.

****

"Oh crap," Larson muttered as he peered around the bend of the corridor leading to the platform's primary exterior exit.

"How many?" Hawks asked, already knowing what Larson must have seen waiting on them.

"At least two dozen," Larson said. "They're not just blocking the door; they're on the ceiling of the corridor too."

"Is there another way out?" Larson asked Riggs and Cheryl.

"Sure," Riggs said, frowning. "If you want to take your chances, either heading down to the lower levels and swim up or make your way back all the way we just came."

"We have to go through them," Hawks replied. "It's the only way."

"And who knows how many more of those things are waiting for us out on the deck if we do fight our way out?" Hyatt argued. "The fighting will surely draw any of those things left on the platform to it."

"Actually, according to the last report from the *Braxton*," Robbie chimed in, "the main deck out there is pretty clear."

"Pretty clear?" Larson asked.

Robbie didn't answer. Instead, he just gave a shrug.

"Your call," Hawks said to Larson.

"We go through," Larson said firmly. "Anybody carrying a grenade?"

"I am," Chuck spoke up.

"Then let's get this show on the road," Larson ordered him.

Chuck removed the grenade from one of the pockets of his vest, pulled its pin, and lobbed it into the corridor where the squid creatures were waiting on them.

"Fire in the hole!" Chuck shouted, ducking back behind the bend in the corridor next to Larson and Hawks.

The ensuing explosion shook the corridor. Black blood and bits of gore were thrown into the corridor where the group was splattered through the air onto its walls and floor.

"Move!" Larson yelled, already charging into the corridor that led to the exterior doorway.

Most of the squid creatures had died in the grenade's blast. Others flopped about on the corridor floor, their tentacles twitching in the death throes that shook their bodies. There were some of the creatures that had only been wounded though, and they rushed forward to meet the members of the advancing group. One of them came straight at Larson. A high-pitched cry arose from its mouth. Larson squeezed his rifle's trigger and sprayed the thing with a stream of automatic fire. The bullets struck its central mass, hurling it backwards as they ripped through it.

Hawks and Chuck took aim at the creatures on the ceiling. They had been the least affected by the blast and came scrambling across it towards the group. Their rifles chattered, blowing squids apart as they advanced. Hyatt shoved his way passed them, careful not to step into their lines of fire. His automatic shotgun thundered in rapid succession as he emptied its magazine into the remaining squid creatures. Larson had seen Hyatt coming and knew what the big man planned to do. He hit the corridor floor in the fraction of a second before the rounds from Hyatt's weapon reduced the last of the squids to pieces of shredded black pulp.

"Keep moving!" Larson shouted as he got back to his feet. Hawks and Chuck darted by him as Hyatt held back to reload.

Hawks and Chuck approached the doorway. A howling wind was blowing rain into the corridor through the opening. It was dark outside. The storm that had the *Braxton* had known was in the area had appeared to finally reach the platform. Hawks squinted, his eyes straining to see clearly in the darkness and rain outside. As far as he could tell, the path ahead was clear.

"Whoa." Chuck caught him by the shoulder as he started forward. "Are we really going out there?"

"You'd rather stay in here?" Hawks asked.

"Good point," Chuck admitted and let go of him.

Larson and Robbie caught up to them at the doorway.

"Robbie, let the *Braxton* know our new count and that we're ready for extraction," Larson ordered.

"Already trying, sir," Robbie answered. "This storm is getting worse and messing with the comms."

"Is that normal?" Riggs and Hawks asked at the same time. The two men looked at each other in surprise.

"No, it most certainly isn't. Not on the level it's happening," Robbie told them.

"Can you get a message through or not?" Larson snapped.

"I think so," Robbie said. "Give me a second."

"I'd say going back down to the boats is out," Hawks commented. "Trying to climb down in those winds would be suicide."

"No kidding," Larson growled. "But we can't stay here either."

"I've gotten through to the *Braxton*, sir!" Robbie called out. "XO Ennis is advising us to hold position until the storm clears."

"Frag that!" Larson snapped even as he looked out at the raging water through the rain and knew the XO was right. Even if there was a copter aboard the *Braxton*, the weather would have made it impossible for it to come for them.

"We need to find somewhere topside that's secure or at least defensible," Hawks said.

"Ha. There ain't anywhere," Riggs chuckled darkly.

"Wait!" Bailey came up to them. "What about our boat, Riggs?"

"The *Hunter*!" Riggs broke into a smile. "I had forgotten all about her."

"You have a boat?" Chuck asked.

"Of course they do, you idiot," Larson snarled, maybe hiding his own stupidity in not thinking to ask. "This is an exploration platform after all."

"If those things haven't destroyed her, the *Hunter* will get us to your battleship. Count on it," Riggs told Larson. "She's a modified small yacht."

"Then why are we all just standing here and getting rained on?" Larson asked. "Lead the way, Riggs."

****

The *Hunter* was moored to the platform's north side. There was a ladder leading down directly onto its deck. The group reached the top of the ladder, standing in the howling wind and being battered by the heavy rain as they looked down at the boat.

"Who's going first?" Hawks asked.

Larson laughed. "I figure that honor belongs to you and Chuck. Get down there and make sure there aren't any of those things aboard her."

"Yes, sir." Hawks flashed a defiant grin at Larson and motioned for Chuck to follow him.

The rungs of the ladder were slick. Hawks and Chuck had to take them carefully with their rifles swung onto their backs. Thankfully, there was no sign of the squid creatures moving about on the boat's deck. The *Hunter* rocked on the angry waves, tossed about by the high winds. Hawks got as close to the deck as he felt he needed and then let go of the ladder dropping onto it. He unslung his rifle as quickly as he could and swept the area about him with his gaze, half-expecting one of the squid creatures to come charging at him from out of the shadows. He heard a thud as Chuck dropped onto the deck behind him.

There was also the threat of the squid creatures in the water scaling the sides of the boat and coming squirming onto its deck, but so far, it looked like the storm had driven them away for the time being.

"You watch out here," Hawks ordered Chuck. "I'll check the cabin."

Hawks moved slowly toward the cabin door. When he reached it, he tried the door and found it unlocked. He threw the door fully open, leveling his rifle at anything that might come bursting out at him. Hawks breathed a sigh of relief as he saw that cabin was clear. He stepped into to it and took a closer look around to be sure before giving Chuck the signal to tell the others to join them.

Chuck and Hawks stood watch against any squid creatures that might decide to brave the storm and attempt to board the boat as the others climbed down. Within a matter of minutes, everyone was ready to roll. Riggs was the only one with experience handling the modified yacht so Larson delegated that duty to him. Hyatt, Bailey, and Cheryl worked to free the boat from its moorings as Robbie sat in the cabin, informing the *Braxton* that they were on their way.

"Take her easy," Larson ordered Riggs from where he stood behind him watching his work.

The *Hunter*'s engine rumbled to life, and Riggs steered the boat away from the platform on course for the *Braxton*. Robbie had given him the coordinates. The *Braxton* was still in its original holding position not far from the platform at all.

The water was as dark and ominous as the skies above the *Hunter* as the small yacht bounced over the waves in route to the large battleship on the horizon. Hawks, Chuck, and Hyatt remained on its deck keeping guard. Everyone else packed into the *Hunter's* small cabin as best they could to take shelter from the storm.

"I still can't believe all this is really happening," Riggs commented without taking his eyes off the waves ahead of the boat.

"Tell me about it," Larson agreed. "I didn't sign up to fight monsters."

"They're not monsters," Bailey argued from where she sat next to Robbie and Cheryl, a towel taken from the boat's stash of supplies wrapped around her shoulders.

"Oh they're monsters alright," Riggs spat. "Those things shouldn't even exist."

"Come on, Riggs," Bailey challenged him. "We know less about the depths of this planet's oceans than we do about space. What gives you the right to say these things shouldn't exist? They're no different than sharks or other predators."

"I watched one of those things gnawing on Brandon's face, Bailey," Riggs snarled. "And I've seen how smart they can be. They're more than just animals no matter how much you want to try to paint them that way."

"That still doesn't make them monsters," Bailey said more quietly. "They're only trying to survive just like we are."

"If you love them that much, Bailey, I can stop this boat right now and let you join them out there," Riggs told her. "How about it?"

The cabin fell silent. Larson looked from Riggs to Bailey. He could feel the tension between the two of them in his bones. Finally, he spoke, breaking the silence. "Look, we're all humans in here, so let's try to remember that, okay?"

The *Hunter* reached the battleship without incident. There was already a group of its crew waiting in place to help them aboard. A ladder was tossed down and Larson made sure that Cheryl was the first one up it. He remembered that she was not only a scientist but also the lady who supposed to have been in charge of the platform before the attack. That made her the most valuable person onboard the *Hunter*. Bailey went up next followed by Robbie. Riggs had to stay to keep the small yacht from losing its position due to the raging waves. Finally, when everyone was up and gone except for Riggs and himself, Larson asked, "You ready?"

Riggs nodded. "I've set her as best I can to hold her position so that we'll have time to get off of her. With this storm though …"

Riggs and Larson left the *Hunter*'s cabin racing through the rain to the rope that dangled down from the side of the *Braxton*.

"After you," Larson told Riggs, shoving the man at the rope. Riggs caught it and started to climb.

A chorus of shrieks arose of the noise of the wind and rain. Larson looked out at the water around the *Hunter*. Dozens of the squid creatures had risen from the waves and attached themselves to the sides of the small yacht. They were pulling themselves up onto it with their tentacles.

"Oh no you don't, you mothers ..." Larson shouted. He took aim at the closest of the squid creatures and popped off a three-round burst that blew chunks out of its central mass and sent the thing toppling back into the waves with a loud splash. Larson saw that were too many of the things to fight and made a break for the rope. Riggs was moving up it slowly. The wind and rain had grown in intensity, making it difficult to climb, even for folks with as much training as Larson and his squad had. Larson could see it was taking everything Riggs had to just to keep his grip on the rope. Those above them on the *Braxton*'s deck had begun to pull the rope up carrying Riggs along with it even as he tried to climb.

Larson ran and jumped, grabbing the end of the rising rope and catching hold of it. He swung wildly through the air as a squid creature that had leaped at him almost snagged his right leg with one of its primary tentacles. The movement of the rope though shook Riggs from it. Larson watched, cursing himself, as Riggs fell to the deck of the *Hunter*. Riggs crashed into it with a heavy thud and lay still in the pooling water gathering on the small yacht's deck from the storm. Riggs' fall was his fault. He knew he couldn't let the man die alone. Larson waited until the swinging of the rope carried him back over the small yacht's deck and let go, aiming his fall. His combat boots thudded onto the wood of the deck next to where Riggs lay. With the deck wet from the rain, his feet slid out from under him. He slammed into the deck, landing on his back as his breath was knocked from his lungs. Larson struggled to breathe as he rolled onto his side and saw one of the squid creatures, its tentacles hauling it along the deck towards him.

His unexpected fall had caused him to lose his rifle, jarring it from his grasp. In the dark and rain, he couldn't see where it had landed and there was no time to hunt for it. Larson reached for his sidearm only to find it gone. He remembered too late he had given it to Riggs. The squid creature was on him before he had a chance to do anything else. The thing's lesser tentacles wrapped themselves around his arms and legs. Larson struggled against them, trying to reach the knife he kept in his boot. They were too strong to break free of though. Larson opened his mouth not to scream but curse the squid creature. As he did so, the spear-like tip of one of its primary tentacles was thrust into his mouth. It ripped teeth from gums and sliced his tongue apart on its way through him. The tip of the tentacle erupted from the backside of his skull in an explosion of blood and flying bone fragments.

Riggs saw it all happening but couldn't move to help Larson. His own fall had broken his neck. He couldn't feel his body, much less move it. Blood had flowed up from inside him to leak over his lips from his mouth. Riggs tried to scream for help, but all that came out was a horrid gargling noise. There was no hope of anyone watching from the side of the *Braxton* above reaching him in time anyway. All his attempt at screaming did was draw the attention of the other squids to him where he lay. They gathered around him, slicing at him with their tentacles. Riggs watched entire chunks of his flesh torn away in their hungry mouths but still felt nothing. One of the squid creatures moved to place its mouth directly above his forehead. Riggs stared up into that maw helpless to do anything to drive it away from him. Then the squid dropped its mouth onto him. The last thing Riggs heard was the crunching sound of his own skull being broken as the squid creature's teeth sunk into it.

****

Chuck had started to open fire on the monsters surrounding the bodies of Riggs and Larson on the deck of the *Hunter*, but Hyatt stopped him.

"No point in that, man," Hyatt said. "They're dead already and you know it. All you'll do is draw their attention up here."

"Robbie!" Hawks shouted. "Tell the Captain to get the *Braxton* underway!"

"Yes, sir!" Robbie answered, fiddling with his tablet.

Hyatt turned to the crewmen who had lowered rope and helped them all get up it. "All of you, stand ready! If those things start trying to climb up here, it's up to us to stop them."

"And not a shot before he says so!" Chuck added, stepping up to stand beside Hyatt.

The *Braxton* started moving. She was a large vessel and took time to build up speed. Hawks kept his eyes fixed on the squid creatures aboard the *Hunter*. They looked too busy enjoying their newly claimed meal of Larson and Riggs to care that the big ship was pulling away. Of course, Hawks knew that any other creatures who might be in the water around the *Braxton* might not be so inclined to let her escape. He was proud of Hyatt for how the big man had taken the initiative in warning the crewmen to be ready in case the squids did try to broad.

"There!" Chuck shouted, pointing toward the aft section of the *Braxton*'s hull. A group of four squids had slapped their tentacles onto the ship there and were beginning to climb up. Hyatt jerked up his automatic shotgun and blasted away at them. The closest of the squids heard his shots and flinched, but all of the creatures including it were too far out of range for Hyatt's weapon to be effective.

"Get some people over there and stop them!" Hawks shouted at the crewmen who appeared to be in command of the others even as he sprinted in the direction of the squids himself. The rain drenching the *Braxton*'s deck made it hard from his to keep his footing as he ran. He tried to stop as he neared the edge of the ship above where the squid creatures were climbing up its hull but couldn't. Hawks slid into the railing with a sharp grunt. He managed to keep his hold on his rifle though. Wincing from the pain where his ribs had struck the railing, he raised his rifle, angling it downwards at the squids. Hawks didn't even try to aim. He snapped his rifle over to fully automatic and hosed the area the squids were clustered in until the weapon clicked empty. Black blood splattered into the air and mixed with the rain on the wind as his rounds hammered the more unlucky of the squid creatures. One of them wailed as it let go of the *Braxton*'s hull and went twisting end over end through the raging storm to splash into the waves below. Another of the squid's lost two tentacles to the stream of fire Hawks had sent their way but somehow it managed to keep its hold on the ship. The two Hawks hadn't hit scrambled upwards along the *Braxton*'s hull so fast they looked like nightmarish giant spiders running across their web to where their prey was trapped.

Two members of the battleship's crew and Chuck joined Hawks at the railing as Hawks struggled to reload his rifle. They opened up on the remaining squids and blew them to bits before Hawks was even able to get his fresh magazine slammed home.

"Clear!" the crewmen next to him yelled back in the direction of Robbie and Hyatt.

"Clear on all sides!" Robbie shouted back after checking the screen of the tablet he clutched. "We need to get inside before they try again!"

"No!" Hyatt contradicted him. "We need people out here to hold those things off until the *Braxton* is able to put some distance between us and them!"

"Roger that!" Robbie yelled back at him over the wind. "I'll let the XO know we're going to need help out here."

Hawks ran to them and grabbed Robbie by his arm. "Not you! I want you inside with the survivors from the platform! Somebody needs to let Captain Weaver know what we're up against out here!"

Robbie nodded. "Yes, sir!"

"Ladies, you're with me!" Robbie shouted at Cheryl and Bailey.

Hawks watched the three of them go as they headed for the closest entrance to the battleship's interior. He wanted to go with them, but he knew that whatever crewmen the XO sent out to hold the squid creatures off were going to need all the help they could get.

****

The *USS Braxton* was well underway now. She was pulling over thirty knots and continuing to build speed. Her CIWS was set to auto and every so often sprang to life, sending a barrage of fire at masses of the squid creatures that got too close. Captain Weaver sat on the edge of his command chair, watching his bridge crew at work around him. The squad of marines and the few survivors from Platform Alpha One were finally onboard and he needed to meet with them very badly. The more he knew about the squid creatures he was up against, the better.

"Ennis," Captain Weaver called to his XO. "You have command until I return."

"Yes, sir," Ennis said, sliding into the command chair as Captain Weaver left it.

Ennis watched the captain leave the bridge. It was disturbing that there were still squid creatures in the water to set off the CIWS. Ennis had figured they were localized around Platform Alpha One. The ship was a good distance from the platform now though and still, it was encountering swarms of the things. There had been no sign of the creatures this far out on their approach to Platform Alpha One. So much was unknown about the creatures and their origins. Ennis hoped Captain Weaver would be able to find out where the things came from and what they were from the survivors. In the meantime, it was up to him to keep the *Braxton* going and safe from the monsters.

Captain Weaver had ordered a course set for the coordinates of DESRON 2. Like the *Braxton* had been before receiving the distress call from the platform, the DESRON was on maneuvers. There was something to be said for safety in numbers, and more firepower was always a good thing. Captain Weaver had made the decision to join up with Surface Commander Hoffman's force after they had seen that the squids were relentless in their pursuit of the ship. They might not be as fast, but the *Braxton*'s sonar confirmed that main swarm of the things were still after the ship, despite how much they had fallen behind it.

A yeoman brought him a mug of coffee. Ennis nodded at the crewmen, thankful for it. He blew on the hot, streaming blackness inside the mug before taking a sip from it. The coffee was strong and black just as he liked it. He hadn't realized just how much of a toll the situation had taken on him until the caffeine started hitting his system.

"Sir," Lancaster called to him from the sonar station. "I think you might want to see this. Contact to aft."

Ennis carried his coffee with him as he got up from the command chair and walked over to where Lancaster sat. "What is it?"

Lancaster shrugged. "I don't know, sir. It might just be some kind of echo but…"

Ennis looked at the image Lancaster was pointing at on the sonar screen.

Barely managing not to spit out the mouthful of coffee he'd just drank, Ennis sat his mug aside and leaned over Lancaster, bringing his eyes closer to the screen. "That's no echo. Look at it. It may be matching the *Braxton*'s movements like a shadow, but it's not doing so perfectly."

"I've run a level-one diagnostic, sir, but the system appears to be operating without any glitches," Lancaster added.

Ennis was having a hard time trusting his own instincts given the size of the thing the sonar was picking up, but they told him that whatever it was, it was alive and after them.

"The squid creatures seem to be giving whatever it is a wide berth," Lancaster told him.

"Don't blame them," Ennis said. "That thing is massive."

"Twice the size of the *Braxton*, sir," Lancaster confirmed. "Surely, it can't be…"

Ennis accepted what his mind didn't want to acknowledge. "It is. It's something like those squid creatures. Some sort of new species we've never seen before and it's after us."

"Sir, it's increasing speed," Lancaster sputtered.

"I can see that," Ennis growled and headed back to the command chair.

"Helm, increase speed," Ennis ordered.

"We're already at maximum, sir," Watkins reminded him.

"Smith," Ennis called out.

"Sir?" the weapons officer answered, sitting up straighter at his station.

"Take the large contact to aft with guns," Ennis ordered.

"Yes, sir," Smith said.

"All batteries," Ennis added.

Smith blinked at the command but went to work targeting the massive aft contact.

The *Braxton*'s main guns that could be angled for such a shot rotated on their turrets to engage the contact. It sounded like a storm ripping unexpectedly across a clear summer sky as they fired. Ennis had called up an image of the area behind the ship on the personal display of the command chair. He watched as explosions hammered the water where the contact was located. In the wake of the explosions, black blood stained the waves rising up from beneath them.

"Direct hit!" Smith shouted.

Ennis nearly lost it at the sight of what happened next. A long, thick tentacle broke through the surface of the water and rose towards the heavens. The thing was half as thick the *Braxton*. It splashed back down angrily into the waves as if whatever it was attached to was flipping the *Braxton* off.

"Again!" Ennis snapped at Smith, leaning forward on the edge of the command chair.

The *Braxton*'s heavy guns fired once more, churning the water with a second round of explosions.

"Contact is changing course and breaking off, sir!" Lancaster shouted.

Ennis slumped back into the command chair. "Did we hurt it?"

"No way to know for sure, sir," Lancaster said, "but from the looks of things, we did."

Ennis agreed with that assessment. The blackness in the water had to be the thing's blood. He knew the squid creatures bled black. The tentacle that had risen up in the wake of the explosions looked very similar to those of the smaller squid creatures. At the very least, they had given the monster pause. Ennis didn't doubt that it would be back, but for now, the volleys from the guns had driven it off.

Captain Weaver had been right to set an intercept course for the nearby DESRON. Ennis didn't relish the idea of facing that thing alone. His gut told him that the monster could make short work of the *Braxton* anytime it felt like it.

Ennis hit the internal intercom button and hailed engineering. "Chief, I understand you guys are doing the best you can down there, but we really need more speed. Do whatever it takes to make that happen."

****

Surface Commander Hoffman sat in his command chair reading over the report his XO, Shooter, had brought him. The *USS Braxton* was in route to their position. Hoffman frowned. Captain Weaver had always struck him as a competent and rational man. The two of them had met several times over the years. He wondered what had happened to Captain Weaver and the *Braxton*, because what the ship's XO had claimed upon contacting DESRON 2 surely couldn't be true. The *Braxton*'s XO had told Hoffman's comm. officer that the ship was under attack by a newly discovered species of squid-like creatures they had encountered while responding to a distress call from a civilian research facility known as Platform Alpha One. There had been no further word from the *Braxton* since that time, but the *Mitchell*'s long-range sensors pegged the ship as still on course and approaching DESRON 2's position at maximum military speed. Hoffman had brought the four ships of DESRON 2 to alert status. His flagship, the *Mitchell*, was at the center of the DESRON's formation. The *Rigel* and *Hercules* flanked her with the *Bonime* bringing up the formation's rear.

There was nothing in the information that his XO had pulled on Platform Alpha One to indicate that any illegal genetic or bio-weapon research had been taking place at the facility. Everything about it checked out on paper. It appeared in every way to be the research and exploration station that the *Braxton*'s XO had reported it being. Hoffman rubbed at his cheeks with his fingers, thinking over the situation. Part of him had worried that the facility had been working on something that might have affected its own crew and then the crew of the *Braxton*. A neural agent or toxin causing a delusional state made more sense than the claims of being attacked by monsters from the depths. This was real life, not some B-grade horror film.

"It's all rather strange, isn't it, sir?" Shooter asked, walking up to stand beside the command chair, a mug of tea in his hand.

Surface Commander Hoffman nodded. "If it were anyone but Weaver out there, I would have laughed it all off as some kind of joke."

"I know," Shooter said. "I've met Captain Weaver too. Never seemed the sort to screw around to me."

"So what in the devil is going on then?" Hoffman asked. "Are we really supposed to believe that there are monsters tough enough to put a U.S. Navy battleship on the run out there?"

"The *Braxton* should reach our position within the hour, sir, so I guess we'll find out soon enough." Shooter shrugged and slurped at his tea.

"What about the storm?" Surface Commander Hoffman asked.

"It's cleared the area, sir," Shooter told him. "However, we're still having trouble with the long-range comm. systems. I've got our best techs on figuring out what's going on with it."

"Good." Hoffman smiled. Shooter was the type of XO that every captain prayed they would get assigned to their command. He took the initiative and got things done, well and right.

"The entire DESRON is on alert too just as you ordered," Shooter added. "If the *Braxton* is bringing trouble with her, we'll be ready for it."

Hoffman chuckled. "Monsters." He said the word like the joke it had to be. "Weaver will have to the luckiest captain alive to keep his command after this. Even if he does, he'll never live this mess down."

"Aye, sir," Shooter agreed, "unless there are really monsters after him of course."

"Don't tell me you believe that crap," Hoffman laughed. As steady as Captain Weaver had seemed the times they had met, even the best men could snap. Hoffman had to admit to himself that a part of him truly believed Weaver's claims but it was so much easier to laugh at it all.

"As you may recall, sir," Shooter said, "I have an interest in marine biology myself. The depths of the Earth's oceans are less explored than space. There have been a lot of strange and mind-boggling lifeforms discovered in its depths over the years. Who's to say that the folks aboard Platform Alpha One didn't find something more than they bargained for in their exploration efforts?"

"Ugly-looking fish, bizarre coral formations, weird fungal light on the ocean floor? That type of stuff I'll buy, Shooter, but monsters? Even coming from someone like Captain Weaver, that still just seems too unlikely. The *Braxton* is a fully armed and combat operational battleship Shooter. There shouldn't be anything alive out there under the waves that could really be a threat to her."

"Ennis claimed these squid creatures can move about out of the water," Shooter told him. "That they boarded ships by climbing their hulls. It would take one heck of a mutation to create creatures like that, sir."

Surface Commander Hoffman grunted, leaning forward in his chair. He looked over at Shooter, shaking his head. "I'll believe it when I see it."

****

Captain Weaver entered the *Braxton*'s medical bay. Both of the women from Platform Alpha One were resting there with Dr. Hall looking after them. Neither of the women had suffered anything more than a bit of exposure and some cuts and bruises. Specialist Robbie from Larson's strike team was there too. Robbie hopped from the chair he was sitting in, coming to attention as he entered the room.

"At ease, son," Captain Weaver told him.

"Did the others make it, sir?" Robbie asked.

Captain Weaver shook his head. "Your CO, Larson, and the man from the platform were both killed by the creatures before they could make it aboard."

"What about Hawks?" the young specialist demanded.

"He's fine, son. Hawks and the rest of your unit led the defense of this ship as those things, squids, whatever they are, tried to board us. Beat them back pretty good too from what I have heard."

"Good to know, sir," Robbie said with a grin.

Captain Weaver had been keeping track of what was going on by listening in on Ennis through the comm. piece he wore inside his right ear. He kindly motioned the young specialist from his path and continued on to where the two women from the platform sat.

"Don't press them too hard," Dr. Hall instructed him. "They've been through a lot in the last bit."

Ignoring Dr. Hall's comment, Captain Weaver moved to stand in front of the two women. "I hear one of you is the captain of Platform Alpha One."

"Not captain, just administrator," the taller woman replied, getting up to offer him her hand. "I'm Dr. Cheryl Drake, and this is Dr. Amanda Bailey."

Captain Weaver accepted her hand, shaking it, surprised by the firmness of her grip. "Welcome aboard the *Braxton*," he said. "I'm sorry it's not under better circumstances."

"Did I hear you correctly that my man, Riggs, is dead?" Cheryl asked.

"Yes," Captain Weaver replied, nodding. "You have my deepest condolences."

Captain Weaver heard Bailey gasp at the news. Cheryl though seemed to take it in stride.

"We've lost so many good people, Captain," Cheryl told him. "Tell me the nightmare is over now."

"Not quite, I'm afraid," Captain Weaver said honestly. "Those creatures have attacked this ship too. As you likely heard, we drove them off, but they'll be back. You can count on that."

"But surely this ship…?" Cheryl started.

"What can you tell me about these creatures?" Captain Weaver interrupted her. He listened intently as both Cheryl and Bailey told what they could. When they were done, Captain Weaver sighed. There was still so much left unanswered.

"There are more than just those things out there," he told them. "While this ship has been underway, in route for a DESRON located on maneuvers nearby, we've encountered something else. From what I'm told, it's massive, larger than this ship."

"The lifeform from the trench!" Dr. Bailey exclaimed. "That had to be what it was."

Cheryl was shaking her head like a woman on the verge of going mad. "It can't be."

"It has to be!" Dr. Bailey argued. "Whatever was down there that we were originally picking up, something has woken it up too."

"The squids..." Cheryl rasped. "If your theory about them being its caretakers, for lack of a better term, is correct, that would make sense. When this ship arrived, those things must have decided they couldn't fully protect the lifeform and their ingrained biological directive at that point was to wake it so it could deal with whatever the threat to it was itself."

"Doctors," Captain Weaver pleaded. "Please. Pretend I have no idea what you're talking about and clue me in as to what we're dealing with."

"Something old," Cheryl told him. "Far older than man."

"I'd wager intelligent too," Dr. Bailey added. "Think of it as an apex predator, Captain; one that's been asleep for millennia that has just woken up to a strange new world. That's what you're facing."

"And it's a squid too? A giant one?" Captain Weaver asked. "That would fit with what my crew saw."

Dr. Bailey was nodding. "Have you heard the term Kraken, Captain?"

"From mythology? Sure. Who hasn't?" Captain Weaver said, frowning.

"It's possible that this thing, or one of its species, was the basis for those myths," Dr. Bailey explained.

"You can't be serious," Captain Weave stammered.

"Deadly so." Dr. Bailey met his eyes. "This thing, Captain … It and its spawn, which is likely what the smaller squid creatures are, isn't going to stop until we're all dead. No matter what you do, it'll keep coming at us until either it is dead or we are."

"She's right," Cheryl chimed in. "Beyond the fact that we invaded its territory, it will see this ship and others like her as a threat to its dominance and one that has to be eliminated at all costs."

"I don't suppose you have any ideas on how to stop it?" Captain Weaver asked.

"It is alive, Captain, and it bleeds just like we do," Cheryl said smugly. "I suggest you shoot it until it is dead."

"Thanks," Captain Weaver's snapped, his sarcasm sharp. "That's a great help. It really is."

"I'm sorry, Captain," Dr. Bailey said with a frown. "There's nothing else we can tell you."

Ennis' voice came over the comm. piece Captain Weaver wore in his ear. "Captain, we've reached DESRON 2. Surface Commander Hoffman would like to speak with you at once, sir."

"Tell him I'll be right there," Captain Weaver said and then looked back at the two women from the platform. "I'm needed on the bridge. I am sure Dr. Hall and Robbie can attend to any needs you may have. If you think of anything else at all about this Kraken we're facing…"

"We'll come to you at once, Captain," Cheryl assured him.

Captain Weaver left the two women staring after him as he raced out of the medical bay.

****

Ennis got up from the command chair as Captain Weaver stepped onto the *Braxton*'s bridge. Captain Weaver took the chair, nodding at the XO.

"Surface Commander Hoffman for you, sir," Ennis told him.

"On speakers," Captain Weaver ordered.

"Captain Weaver," Hoffman's voice filled the bridge. "We're picking up a large number of small contacts just outside the DESRON 2's formation perimeter."

"Yes, sir," Captain Weaver answered. "Those would be the smaller squid creatures that are pursuing us."

"I see," Hoffman said, clearly doubtful that the contacts were what he claimed they were.

"Hoffman," Captain Weaver said earnestly, "I highly suggest that all the ships of DESRON 2 secure their decks and deploy armed personnel in case the creatures decide to engage them."

"Secure the decks?" Surface Commander Hoffman questioned him.

"Yes, sir." Captain Weaver nodded though he knew the surface commander couldn't see him over the audio only commlink. "If they do engage us, sir, they'll try to board, swarming whatever ship or ships they make a go at. If they get into its interior…"

"I understand, Captain Weaver." Hoffman's tone had an edge of warning in it.

Captain Weaver wasn't concerned. If Hoffman didn't believe him, the surface commander would soon learn well enough himself just how real and dangerous the squid creatures were.

"I'll order the precautions you suggest, Captain," Surface Commander Hoffman told him, if somewhat reluctantly.

"Hoffman," Captain Weaver said, "there's something else out there too."

The surface commander was silent, waiting on him to continue.

"Whatever it is, it's massive," Captain Weaver warned. "My XO, Ennis, managed to drive it off when it engaged us in route here, but it wasn't easy. This thing … It is fast, sir, and smart. When it does hit DESRON 2, it'll come in fast and do as much damage as it can. I'll be sending you a full report of what little we know about it in the next half hour."

"See that you do," Surface Commander Hoffman ordered.

Surface Commander Hoffman ended the transmission between the two ships, leaving the bridge of the *Braxton* in silence.

"He doesn't believe a blasted word of what we've told him, sir," Ennis spoke up.

"He will." Captain Weaver glanced over at the XO. "Let's just hope he doesn't get us all killed before he comes around."

"Sir," Lancaster called from the *Braxton*'s sonar station.

"What is it, Lancaster?" Captain Weaver asked. "Has the big one returned?"

Lancaster shook his head. "No, sir, I'm not picking up any sign of it out there yet, but the small ones, sir, they're gathering in force around the perimeter of DESRON 2's formation. I'm picking up over a thousand of them, sir, and more are joining the mass already gathered with each minute that passes."

"They're getting ready for an all-out attack," Ennis said.

"Should I take them with guns, sir?" Smith, the *Braxton*'s weapon officer, asked.

Captain Weaver shook his head. "Not yet, Smith, but get a lock on them anyway."

"Yes, sir." Smith nodded. "I'll be ready."

"Sound action stations," Captain Weaver ordered Ennis.

"Hoffman isn't going to like that, sir," Ennis warned him.

"My ship, my call," Captain Weaver said. "We're not officially part of DESRON 2, Ennis, and I'd rather be ready than not when those things make their move. I don't think we'll have to wait very long at all for them to make it."

****

Major Lewis stood on the deck of the *USS Mitchell*. Surface Commander Hoffman had ordered that he deploy all of his men to defend the flagship should the squid creatures surrounding the DESRON make a move against it. Major Lewis had seen the footage of the monsters that the captain of the *Braxton* had sent over. It was still hard to believe that such creatures existed. The ships of DESRON 2 were too close in their formation for the CIWS of any of them to engage the squid things if they made a direct attempt at boarding. Producing a cigarette from his the pocket of his jacket, Major Lewis lit up. He puffed on it as he watched his second-in-command, Jenkins, getting the men ready. Major Lewis had ordered several SAWs set up at various points along the main deck of the *Mitchell.* They were a secondary line of defense should the squid creatures manage to make it up the sides of the ship and get aboard. Of course, Major Lewis didn't plan on letting the creatures make it that far.

Alarm Klaxons blared not just on the *Mitchell* but aboard the other ships of DESRON 2 as well.

"Contacts inbound!" Tyler, the ship's comm. Officer, informed him over the comm. unit inside his helmet. Major Lewis didn't have time to ask how many of the things he could expect before all hell broke loose. The men he had stationed along the sides of the ship opened up with their rifles, firing downward, over the ship's railing, at the waters below. Major Lewis rushed to join the closest group of his men. Jenkins followed after him. Major Lewis reached the port side of the *Mitchell* to see dozens upon dozens of the squid creatures slapping their tentacles onto the side of the ship and pulling themselves up out of the waves. They came scampering up the side of the ship like crazy-looking spiders. He watched as fire from his men tore at their ranks. One squid took numerous hits to its central mass and exploded in a burst of black blood and gore. Another took a burst that caused it to lose its hold on the side of the ship and tumble back into the water below. Still another had one of its primary tentacles blown completely from its body by one of his men packing a high-powered shotgun. The creature shrieked as the stump of its tentacles sprayed black blood, flopping about madly in the air, before another of his men finished it with a stream of fully automatic rifle fire that ripped its central mass to shreds.

For all the effort his men were putting into sending the things back to whatever Hell they had crawled out of, the squid creatures were just too fast and too many. The first of them reached the ship's railing and lashed out with one of its primary tentacles even as his man carrying the shotgun blew it apart. That single swipe of its tentacles took the head off the shoulders of one of his men and knocked another from his feet with his right arm barely still attached to his body by a few strands of muscle and sinew. Three more the things reached the top of the *Mitchell*'s portside hull and flung themselves over the railing onto the deck. They too died quickly as his men concentrated their fire on them, but one of the things managed to spear his man carrying the shotgun through his chest. The soldier's eyes went wide in horror as the tentacle that impaled him wriggled about within him and he knew he was dead. Blood flowed up and out of the man's mouth as his body went limp upon the tentacle that was sticking through him. The squid thing flung the dead soldier's body over the edge of the ship even as it too died from several bursts of point-blank fire from the other soldiers surrounding it. Those three squids were really nothing more than a distraction to keep his men from continuing to defend the side of the deck. In the brief moment it took to eliminate them, half a dozen more were over the railing after them.

"Fall back!" Major Lewis shouted at the few men near him who were still alive. The squid creatures were having their vengeance full-on now that they had reached the deck and closed to melee range. Tentacles slashed open throats, guts, and faces as other tentacles crushed and snapped bones. By the time he, Jenkins, and the two other survivors of the overwhelmed unit got behind the covering fire of the nearest SAW, there were at least forty of the squid creatures on the deck along the port side of the *Mitchell*. The heavy SAW chattered pouring fire into them, cutting half of them down like a scythe sweeping through a field of barley. It wasn't enough though. The other twenty or so squid creatures came crashing into the ranks of his men around the SAW, making short work of them. Major Lewis ignored the screams of his dying men as he fought on.

Someone or something shoved him roughly to the deck. Major Lewis slammed into it with a grunt, rolling over to bring the barrel of his weapon level with the squid that had struck him. He held the trigger of his weapon tight, emptying half of its magazine into the squid. The bullets reduced the squid creature that hit him to little more than black-smeared pulp, sending chunks of its body flying. What remained of its corpse flopped on top of him. Major Lewis shoved the squid off of him and leaped to his feet just in time to see Jenkins lifted into the air by one of the squid creatures. One the creature's tentacles was wrapped about Jenkins' throat, the other around one of his legs. With a sharp jerk, the squid creature yanked Jenkins' leg from his body. A muffled, strangled attempt at a scream came from Jenkins before the squid creature began to sling his body around in a circle above it by the hold it still had around his throat. Major Lewis was close enough to hear Jenkins' neck snap as the squid flung him around before finally tossing him over the side of the ship.

The loud cacophony of gunfire that had sprung up all over the *Mitchell*'s deck was dying out. Major Lewis could hear only a few scattered batches of automatic weapons' chatter left. He knew the battle for the ship was lost. The squid had fully overrun his men and were now working at tearing at the doors that led into the flagship's interior corridors.

Major Lewis had spent most of his adult life as a soldier. He always knew he would die in combat and today looked to be that day. If the squids reached the *Mitchell*'s interior, all was lost. Surface Commander Hoffman wouldn't have enough personnel left to hold the monsters at bay and run the ship too. Major Lewis made his choice without hesitation. He dug the grenade he had slipped into his one of his jacket's pockets out and pulled its pin. With a berserker like battle cry he ran straight into the cluster of squids attacking the doors. The flash of the explosion was the last thing he saw as the grenade blew him and a good number of the squids he had charged into to bits.

****

Surface Commander Hoffman and Shooter, his XO, watched the massacre of Major Lewis and his men on the *Mitchell*'s deck outside. Lewis and his men had killed a staggering number of the squid creatures, but the engagement had still been so one-sided and brief that massacre seemed the only word to describe it.

"They'll get in," Shooter told him. "Those doors aren't going to hold them."

Surface Commander Hoffman looked over at the XO and knew Shooter was right.

"Contact!" the *Mitchell*'s sonar tech, Robinson, shouted. "Something very large and very fast is approaching the DESRON from the south at over thirty-five knots."

Surface Commander Hoffman's head whipped about at the sound of Robinson's voice.

His XO, Shooter, was already racing towards the sonar station. Surface Commander Hoffman saw Shooter quickly double check the data from sonar before saying, "It's the big one that Captain Weaver mentioned, sir. There's no doubt about it. It appears to be on approaching the *Bonime* at ramming speed!"

"Order all ships to take the new contact with guns!" Surface Commander Hoffman shouted from his command chair.

"The *Rigel* is reporting that she's been overrun like we have, sir!" Shooter shouted back at him. "The squids have penetrated her interior and Captain Travis is requesting immediate assistance!"

"Tell him he's just going to have to hold on," Surface Commander Hoffman growled, still waiting to hear the sound of the ships of DESRON 2 bringing their main guns to bear on the approaching giant monster. It was the *Bonime* that fired first. Her main guns thundered and CIWS flashed, sending orange tracer rounds slashing across the waves. The *Hercules* joined the *Rigel*, blasting away at the approaching contact with everything she had. The *Braxton* was the last to start firing, but even she added her firepower towards the inbound contact.

"Why aren't we firing?" Surface Commander Hoffman screamed at his weapons officer, Rickman.

"Main power has gone offline, sir!" Rickman shouted. "Even the CWIS is down!"

"God help us!" Surface Commander Hoffman heard Shooter wailing as the entrance doors to the bridge crashed inward, knocked from their frame to clatter onto the floor.

Surface Commander Hoffman stared into the almost glowing red eyes of the first squid creature that came through the broken doorway. There were two security officers on the bridge. They moved toward the thing to engage it, drawing the weapons holstered on their hips. The pistols cracked over and over as they poured fire into the monster. It shrieked a series of high-pitched wails as they peppered its body with bullet holes that leaked black blood before the monster finally flopped over onto the floor. Unfortunately, there were dozens more creatures coming through the doorway behind it. They entered the bridge, spreading out as they did so, their tentacles lashing outwards toward anyone unlucky enough to be near them. Surface Commander Hoffman watched Rickman die, the spear-like tip of a tentacle driving its way home into his right eye and out the backside of his skull.

Having no weapon, all Surface Commander Hoffman could do was retreat towards the bridge's window. Shooter had taken to carrying a sidearm since the threat of the squid creatures had become known. The XO moved himself to stand between Surface Commander Hoffman and the advancing mass of squids that killed the bridge crew one by one as they closed in on the two of them.

"It's been an honor serving with you, sir!" Shooter cried out as his pistol bucked in his hands as he fired repeatedly into the central body of the closest squid creature. To his credit, Shooter killed the thing before the others swarmed over him and the XO vanished from Surface Commander Hoffman's sight beneath a writhing mass of tentacles.

Surface Commander Hoffman heard the bridge's window behind him shatter. Shards of glass rained over him as several tentacles latched onto his body and pulled him apart limb from limb. He barely had time to scream before death claimed him.

****

Captain Henry Newman sat in his command chair on the bridge of the *Bonime*. His knuckles were white from the pressure of his grip on its arms.

"Multiple direct hits!" his weapons officer, Stark, reported.

"No change in the contact's course," Winn, the sonar tech, called from her station. "It hasn't even slowed down, sir."

There was no room in DESRON 2's formation, much less time, for the *Bonime* to engage in evasive maneuvers.

"Keep firing!" Captain Newman ordered. He stood up to peer out the bridge's forward window. He could see the contact speeding through the waves towards his ship. It left streams of black blood in its wake as fire, from all the ships of the DESRON that could, continued to slam into it. *Nothing could take that much damage and keep coming*, Captain Newman thought, *but if anything, whatever was beneath the waves had increased its speed.*

An explosion to starboard drew his attention away from the inbound contact. It came from the direction of the *Rigel*. He looked to see a second explosion shake the *Rigel*. Squid-like creatures swarmed all over the battleship's sides and deck. He had overheard enough of the transmission between the *Rigel* and the *Mitchell* to know that the things were inside her as well. The creatures or the *Rigel*'s crew in their desperate fight to hold the things off must have hit something vital within the ship. Still more explosions ripped all along the length of the *Rigel*. Captain Newman knew she was lost and his own ship would soon be joining her. None of the squid creatures had attacked the deck of the *Bonime* and Captain Newman knew why. The big one had claimed her for its own, and the smaller squid creatures were smart enough to stay out of the thing's way.

"Contact status?" Captain Newman snapped at Winn.

"Impact in seventy seconds!" Winn answered.

"Stark?" Captain Newman said.

"Still hitting it with everything we have, sir." The fear in Stark's voice was clear. Captain Newman knew everything they had wasn't going to be enough. The thing closing on them was just too massive.

"Impact in five... four... three..." Winn started counting down.

There was nothing Captain Newman could do but hope the *Bonime* could survive the hit.

"Impact!" Winn shouted but nothing happened.

Captain Newman's heart had skipped a beat at Winn's warning. He breathed a sigh of relief before the confusion and panic overtook him.

"Where did it go?" he heard his XO, Bryson, yelling at Winn.

Winn was frantically checking the sonar data. "I don't know, sir," she said at first and then swung her head sharply in Bryson's direction. "It's gone under, sir! It's directly below us!"

"What the...?" Bryson started.

The *Bonime* lurched upwards out of the water as something smashed into its lower hull. The *Bonime* dropped back into the water with a massive splash. The impact knocked Captain Newman into his command chair. He was lucky compared to Bryson and many of the others. Bryson was sent flying into weapons station. Stark narrowly avoided being crushed by Bryson as the big man's body flew passed him. The screens of the weapons station shattered as Bryson struck them and then bounced to roll across the floor of the bridge, leaving a trail of blood in his wake.

A power surge rippled through the bridge's systems. The comm. station erupted in a shower of sparks and flames. Ross, the comm. officer, wailed as she leaped up from her seat, her arms and hair on fire. A nearby crewman grabbed her, knocking her to the floor, as he shrugged off his jacket, trying to use it to smother the flames cooking her flesh.

"Medic!" several of the injured bridge crew screamed as they rushed to attend those who had been hurt by the impact.

"Winn!" Captain Newman shouted. "The contact?"

"Still beneath us, sir!" she told him. "I'm not getting a clear reading on it though. I think it may have somehow attached itself to us!"

"Oh God, have mercy on us," Captain Newman muttered as he saw the two massive tentacles rising up over the port and starboard sides of the *Bonime*. They dropped onto the ship, shaking the bridge once more, as they wrapped around it. Captain Newman heard the creaking of metal on the verge of buckling and giving way as the tentacles tightened around the ship. Metal screamed as it ripped and caved inward.

The batch of the *Bonime*'s onboard ordinance detonated. The explosion shook the ship. Flames leaped skyward as pieces of the hull spun away in the blast. It was far from the only explosion. A second erupted towards the ship's aft section as others ripped along her at midship. Stations blew out all around the bridge. The forward window shattered raining glass over those near it. An officer cried out as a shard of glass buried itself in his back between his shoulders before being flung to the floor of the bridge as the *Bonime* shook again.

Captain Newman's XO lay dead not far from his command chair. A piece of the bridge's ceiling had collapsed, nearly severing the man's head as it had struck him. His body twitched as blood pooled around his body.

"Abandon ship!" Captain Newman shouted, but he knew it was too late even as he gave the order. If anyone could reach the lifeboats, that *thing* was still out there, its tentacles still squeezing the *Bonime* as she burned.

Another explosion knocked Captain Newman from his command chair. He landed hard on the floor, his hands plunging into blood and glass to catch himself. He ignored the pain of the glass shards shoved into his palms by his own weight and scrambled to his feet. Through the shattered forward window of the bridge, he looked into the gigantic, yellow eyes of the Kraken as the monster's head rose over the front of the *Bonime*'s bow. He wanted to scream, to run away, but he was so awestruck by those eyes that he froze in his tracks.

The *Bonime* lurched as the Kraken tugged her downwards beneath the waves. Her bow went down first, raising her aft section skyward. Captain Newman was picked up by the sudden rush of water that poured through the smashed bridge window. It carried him along, slamming him into the rear wall of the bridge. Water rushed into his open mouth and flooded his lungs as the rush of the water held him where he was. And then there was only blackness as the world spun around him and his eyes closed a final time.

****

Captain Weaver watched as the Kraken pulled the *USS Bonime* below the waves. It was like seeing something out of a Verne novel come to life before his eyes. The *Bonime* was burning as the Kraken dragged her down. Numerous explosions had blown holes in her hull and tendrils of black smoke rose from her towards the heavens. Then she was simply gone.

The *Mitchell* was gone as well. She had lit up the waves in a flash of heat and light that had sent debris flying as she blew apart. The *Rigel* was sending out distress calls from not only her bridge but several of her decks where crewmen were holed up trying to hold off the squid creatures that were running rampant through her. So far, the *Hercules* appeared to be holding on with minimal damage. Her captain, Nicholson, had taken the warning he'd been given to heart. Captain Newman was glad that at least someone had truly listened to him and believed. Nicholson had sealed all the entrances to the *Hercules'* interior and welded them shut. In addition, he had wisely positioned what troops he had at his disposal to ensure none of the squids would be entering, at least not easily, through the ship's windows. Captain Nicholson had even had the foresight to move his command to the *Hercules'* to a make-shift secondary bridge in her engineering section behind closed bulkhead doors. That was something he hadn't even thought of doing himself. If they got out of this mess alive, Captain Weaver promised himself that whatever report he wrote would include mention of just how capable Captain Nicholson was.

"Open a channel to all ships of the DESRON," Captain Weaver ordered.

"Channel open, sir," his comm. officer replied.

"This is Captain Weaver of the *USS Braxton*. The *Mitchell* has been lost and Surface Commander Hoffman with her. As of now, I am assuming command of all still-functioning ships of DESRON 2."

No reply beyond more cries for help came from the *Rigel*, but Captain Nicholson responded at once acknowledging his command.

The first order of business was to decide what to do about the situation aboard the *Rigel*. Captain Weaver knew any boarding boats he dispatched to go to her aid would never reach her. The waters around the ships of the DESRON were so infested with the smaller squid creatures that the sonar couldn't even give an accurate count of them anymore. But the real worry was the Kraken itself. If the *Braxton* and the *Hercules* lingered in an attempt to aid the *Rigel*, the odds were that they would suffer a similar fate to what had already happened to the *Mitchell* and the *Bonime*. That was something he couldn't afford to risk, no matter how much he wanted to help those left alive aboard the *Rigel*. *The cold, hard truth*, he came to accept as he thought things over, *was they were on their own.*

"Engines at full, Mr. Watkins!" Captain Weaver snapped.

"Yes, sir," Watkins barked from where he sat at the helm.

"Order the *Hercules* to follow our lead. We're getting the hell out of here," Captain Weaver shouted at Ennis.

"I can't believe we're running, sir," Ennis stared at him. "What about the *Rigel*?"

"What other choice do we have?" Captain Weaver shrugged. "As to the *Rigel,* God help those aboard her."

****

Spent shell casings flew from the side of the heavy SAW clattering to the floor of the corridor as Lumley hosed the advancing squid creatures with a continuous stream of bullets. The barrage tore and ripped squid flesh, sometimes blowing entirely through the first squid they struck to dig into the squid behind it. The floor of the corridor was littered with the twitching bodies of dying squid creatures and slicked with the black greasy substance that was their blood. The squid creatures kept coming though, seemingly oblivious to the fate of their brethren who lay dead and the losses they were taking. There was no sign of their attack lessening. It was as if their numbers were without limit.

Lumley was caught in a fighting retreat along with Simmons and his CO, Zek. The three of them had survived the massacre on the *Rigel*'s main deck and fled into the ship's interior. Lumley wondered if Zek had any clue where they were heading to. There weren't that many places left to run to if there were any at all. The squid creatures appeared to be everywhere inside the ship. All the three of them could do was stay on the move and keep killing the things as they showed themselves.

"Check your corners!" Zek was shouting over the thunderous gunfire. "Check your corners!"

The *Rigel*'s main power was failing. The corridors were lit solely by the red glow of emergency backup power. The lights flickered on and off at random intervals, casting shadows throughout the corridors they were running through and making it easier for the squids to get the drop on them as they went.

When they had first fled into the ship, there had been five surviving members of their unit. Love had bought it as they had rounded a corner and one of the creatures had ambushed him there. The thing had slashed his head in half with a single swipe of one of its primary tentacles. Lumley could still see the splatter of brain matter, blood, and bone fragments flying as the man's skull had been sliced open. Paul had died in just as grizzly manner. One of the squid creatures had been lying in wait, clinging to the ceiling of a corridor. It had dropped onto Paul from above him, its primary tentacles plunging into him, one through each side of his chest. The squid creature had torn Paul's upper body apart in an explosion of gore as it jerked the tentacles in opposite directions. The worst part of their deaths to Lumley was that they hadn't been able to retrieve their bodies. They had been forced to leave their fellow soldiers behind to be feasted upon by the squids.

Lumley knew beyond the shadow of a doubt now that the squids did indeed eat those they killed. He'd seen it with his own eyes. Love and Paul had become squid food and that disturbed him far more than their deaths. It scared the crap out of him. Lumley swore that he would never let that happen to him. He felt the bulge of the grenade in the pocket of his jacket and knew what he was going to do if it looked like the squids were going to get him too.

The trio had reached a junction in the *Rigel*'s internal corridors. Simmons, who had found himself on point, paused.

"Which way?" he shouted at Zek.

Zek shook his head. "How in the devil am I supposed to know? Just pick the one that doesn't look to have any squids!"

As if the creatures had somehow heard and understood him from wherever they were hiding in the shadows, they dropped from the ceiling of the corridor on the right and began scurrying along its floor towards them. Zek swept the barrel of his rifle in their direction and fired a few quick bursts into their ranks as Simmons charged into the corridor on the left. Zek followed after him, with Lumley continuing to bring up the rear. As Lumley entered the corridor to the left, the group of squids bounding up the corridor to the right joined up with the group already pursuing them. Lumley kept firing, his SAW growing hotter in his hands. The heavy weapon was almost out of ammo and he had no extra belts for it on him. He had used them all already.

Something flew through the air beside his face as Zek yelled, "Grenade!"

Lumley threw himself flat against the corridor wall as Zek and Simmons found cover farther along the corridor they were in behind him. The explosion shook the whole area, sending bits of squid creatures splattering everywhere. Lumley felt the black blood of the squid splash over him. He broke away from where he had pressed his body to the wall, thankful that he hadn't been hurt by the shrapnel flung about by the detonating grenade and hosed the squids behind those that had been blown apart with the last of his SAW's belt. The heavy weapon clicked empty. He flung it aside, unslinging his rifle from where it hung on his back by its strap.

"Run!" he heard Zek screaming at him. As if on autopilot, Lumley whirled about, turning his back on the remaining squid creatures and sprinted after Zek and Simmons.

"This way!" Simmons shouted leading them into the large, open area of the ship's mess. Lumley nearly gagged from the smell that hung in the air of the room as they entered it. The area was clear of squids, but it was far from empty. There were human corpses everywhere. It looked as if the squids had been dragging any kills that they didn't eat on the spot into the mess and storing them there for later.

Zek was struggling to close the mess's door as Lumley ran through it. Simmons had collapsed onto his knees and was busy vomiting onto the red-slicked floor of the mess.

"Help me!" Zek ordered him. Lumley joined his CO, and between the two of them, they managed to get the door's hatch closed and locked before the squids in the corridor reached it. Seconds after they had closed the doors, they heard the squids slam into it. The mad pounding of their tentacles shook the thick metal door in its frame.

"It won't hold them for long," Lumley told Zek.

"What...?" Simmons started to say as another dry heave hit him. When he recovered from it, he finished, "What are they doing with all these people?" he rasped.

Neither Zek nor Lumley answered him. Lumley was watching the mess door for the squids to break through it. Zek ran across the mess, searching for another way out of it, disappearing into its kitchen area.

Simmons wiped at his lips with the back of his hand as he staggered to his feet. "What in the hell are we going to do, Lumley?"

Lumley had no answer. He just stared into Simmons' haggard face, seeing his own fear reflected in Simmons' eyes.

A burst of gunfire erupted from the kitchen area followed by the sound of Zek screaming. Both he and Simmons turned towards the kitchen area as half a dozen squids came charging out of it at them. Lumley knew that Zek was dead. He had to be, and soon, they would be too.

Simmons jerked his rifle at the squids only to have it click empty. He was closer to the kitchen area than Lumley was so the squids reached him first. One lashed out at Simmons' legs, knocking him from his feet as another bounded on top of him. Simmons writhed beneath it as its mouth ripped away most of his left shoulder. Lumley watched as Simmons tried for his sidearm, having lost his rifle as he fell. Simmons managed to get the weapon clear of its holster but never got the chance to use it. Even as Simmons raised it up towards the squid on him, the creature stabbed one its tentacles through his heart, killing him instantly. Simmons pistol slid from his fingers to clatter onto the floor.

Lumley knew he couldn't fight all six squids by himself. He'd never be able to stop them all in time before they were on him. He threw his rifle at the closest of the things as it sprang at him, yanking the grenade in his jacket out. He pulled its pin, clutching it to him, as the squids fell on him in mass.

The explosion that followed brought an end to Lumley and the six squids alike.

****

Stern looked about at the dozens of wounded filling the *Rigel*'s engineering section. At first, the engineering section had become a sort of field hospital for the crewmen and soldiers trying to hold the squids at bay. Now, the battle outside it was over, and the squids had won. The *Rigel* belonged to them. Stern and Dr. Beck had managed to seal off the section, closing the heavy bulkheads meant to protect it from fire and flooding. The two of them were the only uninjured crewmen left in engineering and maybe on the whole of the *Rigel*. The bulkhead doors were too thick for them to hear the squids on the other side that were surely trying to force their way inside to get at them. That at least was a blessing. There was more than enough fear to go around without those noises adding to it.

Dr. Beck had abandoned his care of the wounded to try the radio gear they had brought with them again. The doctor sat hunched over it, crying out, "This is Dr. Beck aboard the *USS Rigel*. We are in immediate need of extraction. I say again, we are in immediate need of extraction!"

Stern could tell from Dr. Beck's expression that no one was answering him. In truth, for all they knew, the squids had done the same kind of damage to the other ships of DESRON 2 that they had aboard the *Rigel*. It could very well be that there was no one left to come to their aid.

"Give it up, Doc," Stern urged him.

Dr. Beck looked up at him with tear-filled eyes. "It can't end like this," Beck wept openly. "My family needs me."

"We all got family back home, Doc," Stern said coldly. "That don't matter squat to those squid things out there."

"Surely there has to be something we can do," Dr. Beck pleaded.

"Yeah," Stern said. "Sit here and wait on those monsters to figure out a way to get in here."

"They can't get in!" Dr. Beck snapped, flinging the radio gear away from him and standing up.

"Those things are smart, Doc," Stern reminded him. "Given enough time, they'll find a way in. You can count on that. Even if they don't... The *Rigel* is sinking."

"What?" Dr. Beck's eyes bugged. "How can you know that?"

"I can feel it, Doc," Stern told him. "Can't you?"

The two men stared at each other in silence as the moans of the wounded around them filled the void left by their words.

Finally, Stern spoke up again. "Look, Doc, we're dead men. The only thing left we've got to decide is how we're going to go out."

"What do you mean?" Dr. Beck croaked.

"I mean, I know how to set those engines to blow," Stern told him.

"You can't be serious," Dr. Beck spat. "That's insane!"

"Is it, Doc?" Stern growled. "If we blow this ship, think about how many of those monsters we take with us. It might just be enough to make a difference for another ship still fighting out there."

"I won't allow it." Dr. Beck stepped between Stern and the engine controls. Dr. Beck pointed at the wounded men and women around them. "These people are under my care. I won't let you kill them out of some warped need to get vengeance on those things out there."

"That's too bad, Doc," Stern said. "I sort of liked you."

"What do you mean by that?" Dr. Beck asked as Stern lifted his rifle and squeezed its trigger.

Dr. Beck stumbled backwards as the bullet Stern fired slammed into him, turning his chest into a jagged mess of ruptured flesh.

Stern stepped over Beck's body as he moved towards the main controls. He quickly set them to overload the engine and took a seat to wait for death to come calling.

****

The *USS Braxton* raced over the waves, her engines at full military power. The *Hercules* followed her. The two ships were the only survivors of DESRON 2. The DESRON's flagship, the *Mitchell,* along with the *Bonime*, had been destroyed by the great Kraken and its lesser spawn. The *Rigel*, boarded and overrun by the spawn, had been left behind. That fact haunted Captain Nicholson. He understood why Captain Weaver was forced to leave the *Rigel* to the squids, but doing so didn't make it any easier. He wished there had been something, anything, that they could have done to help those trapped aboard her.

His XO, Grant, must have noticed his scowling expression because he walked over and said, "There was nothing anyone could do."

"I know," Captain Nicholson replied.

"Frankly, sir, your taking Captain Weaver at his word when the *Braxton* arrived is all that saved our lives."

Captain Nicholson feigned a smile. "It's not over yet."

Turning to his sonar tech, Keogh, Nicholson asked, "Do you have a reading on the Kraken?"

Captain Nicholson hated calling the giant monster that. He was a practical sort of man with a great deal of combat experience under his belt. To think that he was now up against something straight out of myth bothered him to no end. Such monsters shouldn't exist in the real world. There was enough evil to go around already.

"No, sir," Keogh said, shaking his head. "I haven't been able to pick it up at all since it took the *Bonime* under."

"Keep trying," Captain Nicholson ordered. "We can't afford to have it sneak up on us."

"Yes, sir," Keogh answered. "I can tell you the small creatures are still after us. How they are keeping up, I don't know, but they are."

"Understood," Captain Nicholson ordered.

"Shouldn't we be firing on them, sir?" Grant asked him.

"Maybe." Captain Nicholson shrugged. "But Captain Weaver isn't and hasn't ordered us to do so. Their numbers seem limitless, and we have seen with our own eyes just how little any losses we inflict on them appear to mean. The things are relentless. Besides, the ordnance we have aboard ship isn't as limitless as those things seem to be. If we run into the Kraken again, we'll need everything we have for it and likely then some."

"It's hard to believe, isn't it, sir?" Grant asked.

Captain Nicholson looked over at him. "What's that, Grant?"

"That a bloody squid, no matter how big it may be, just trashed an entire, modern DESRON," Grant told him. "I read a lot of stories as a kid about monsters like it, but they were all set in the old days when sailors depended upon the wind and stars and their boats were made of wood."

Captain Nicholson didn't know how to respond, so he changed the subject. "Are the decks still clear?"

Grant nodded. "Major Larka and his men were able to clear them during the attack on the DESRON before we followed the *Braxton* out of the kill zone. So far, none of the lesser squids have attempted to engage us again."

Captain Nicholson scratched at the stubble on his chin. He looked out the bridge's forward window at the setting sun on the horizon. The day had been nightmarishly long. He was exhausted, but there was no time for sleep until he knew his ship and crew were safe. The weather was clear, and he could already see traces of the night stars among the dying rays of the sun. He wondered if the monsters out there chasing after them felt tired too. If the creatures did, there was no sign of it.

"Peart," Captain Nicholson called to his comm. officer, "are the long-range comms still offline?"

Peart jerked up in his seat at the comm. station. "Yes, sir. I've run every diagnostic I can think of, Captain, and they all suggest our system is fine. Something out there is jamming us. That's my best guess at least."

"Any ideas on who or what might be doing it?" Captain Nicholson asked.

Peart shook his head.

"Captain," Grant spoke up. "Our comm. problems started when the squids arrived. What if they're behind the interference?"

"That would make sense, Grant, but how?" Captain Nicholson said.

"I'm not a scientist, sir," Peart said, "but what if the squids are emitting some sort of signal among themselves to communicate with each other and the Kraken? That signal coming from something the size of the Kraken might be enough to overpower our own and shut it down."

Captain Nicholson frowned. "I hate to say it, but that makes sense. Peart, touch base with Captain Weaver's comm. officer and let them know about your theory."

Peart nodded. "Right away, sir."

Turning back to Grant, Nicholson continued to frown. "Until we get the mess with the comm. sorted, it looks like we're on our own."

"We've been in tough spots before, sir," Grant said, trying to sound reassuring but failing terribly.

"Captain!" Keogh yelled at him. "I've picked up the Kraken, sir!"

"Where?" Captain Nicholson snapped.

"It's coming in from behind us, sir, closing at forty knots." Keogh had gone pale as he made his report.

"Someone has to survive this," Captain Nicholson muttered quietly.

Grant must have heard him because he met his eyes and gave a nod as if he knew what Nicholson was thinking.

"Time to intercept?" Captain Nicholson barked.

"Four minutes at the thing's current speed, sir," Keogh informed him.

"Our engines are already right at the redline," Grant said. "We can't force anymore out of them without running the risk of overloading them and having them burn out."

"Mr. Malkin, bring us about," Captain Nicholson ordered his helmsman.

"Sir?" Malkin asked in disbelief and shock.

"You heard me, Mr. Malkin," Captain Nicholson growled. "Peart, contact Captain Weaver and let him know that we'll be buying him some time."

Fear hung over the crew of the *Hercules* like the building charge of energy in a summer sky before lightning flashed through it. Captain Nicholson knew none of his crew would challenge him on what he was about to do. They were all professionals and were well aware of their duty.

"Captain Weaver for you, sir," Peart said.

"Put him on," Captain Nicholson said.

"Weaver, what in the devil do you think you're doing?" Captain Weaver's voice boomed over the bridge's speakers.

"You know exactly what I am doing," Captain Nicholson answered calmly.

"Turn the *Hercules* around right now, Nicholson. There is no need for this," Captain Weaver roared.

"You're wrong, Weaver," Captain Nicholson told him. "Someone has to survive all this."

"We have a better chance of that together," Captain Weaver argued.

Captain Nicholson shook his head though he knew Captain Weaver couldn't see him. The transmission was audio only. "I don't see it that way." Captain Nicholson leaned forward in his command chair. "That thing out there just ripped its way through DESRON 2 like it was nothing. Tell me, Weaver, do you really think that our two ships can handle it alone?"

Silence hung over the bridge of the *Hercules* as Captain Nicholson waited on Captain Weaver's answer. Captain Weaver dodged the question though.

"I am ordering you to turn the *Hercules* around, Nicholson. I need you with us," Captain Weaver growled.

"What you need is time to get the hell out of here and I am going to get it for you," Captain Nicholson replied and then signaled for Keogh to kill the transmission.

"That went better than it could have," Grant chuckled. "At least he didn't threaten to have us all court-martialed."

Captain Nicholson didn't point out that it was because Captain Weaver was already writing them off as dead and the ship lost.

"So we're really doing this then?" Grant asked.

Laughing darkly, Captain Nicholson smiled and got down to business.

"Time to intercept?" he asked Keogh.

"Two minutes, sir," Keogh seemed to have grown even paler.

"Mr. Grant, assume control of the weapons station please," Captain Nicholson ordered. He had known Grant for a long, long time, and the XO was the best gunner he had ever met.

"Yes, sir," Grant said, relieving the on-duty officer to slide into the chair at the weapons station.

"Take the contact behind with guns, Mr. Grant," Captain Nicholson ordered, "and let's send that thing back to whatever depths of Hell it came from."

"With pleasure, sir," Grant replied with a grin.

****

The *Hercules* came about in the water, slowing her speed. She faced the oncoming Kraken as she brought her guns to bear on the monster. The CIWS sprang to life first, spraying the waves with a virtual wall of lead. It thundered as it spat burst after burst. Her massive Mark 7 guns fired next, followed by her secondary batteries. Bullets ripped the surface of the ocean as sixteen-inch, armor-piercing shells followed them into the depths. Great geysers of black-tinted water splashed upwards as the shells hit their target and exploded. It was as if Hell itself had opened up in waves above and around the Kraken. Still, the great beast came onward without so much as slowing its speed.

"Keep firing!" Captain Nicholson ordered Grant. "Empty everything we have into that bastard!"

The *Hercules* continued its barrage as the Kraken drew ever closer to her.

"The Kraken has increased its speed to forty-five knots!" Keogh shouted.

That's ramming speed, Captain Nicholson thought but said nothing aloud. Most of his crew would surely come to the same conclusion. "Mr. Grant, target the Kraken's main body."

"I have been, sir," Grant rasped.

"I think the thing is using its lesser tentacles as shields, sir," Keogh yelled.

"Any change in course?" Captain Nicholson demanded to know.

"None, sir," Keogh answered him. "Impact in less than one minute."

"Evasive maneuvers!" Captain Nicholson ordered his helmsman. "Engines at full!"

"She's almost through our kill zone, sir," Grant told him. "Once that thing clears it, only the CIWS will be able to keep firing."

"The Kraken has cleared the kill zone, sir," Keogh shouted. "It's increased speed again to forty-eight knots!"

Captain Nicholson blinked at Keogh's report of the Kraken's speed. Surely he had to have heard the sonar tech wrong; nothing that big could move that fast through the waves.

The *Hercules'* main guns fell silent as her CIWS thundered on.

"Dear God," Grant stammered. "How is that monster still alive?"

Captain Nicholson had no answer. The amount of damage the Kraken had to have taken was staggering and surreal. By all rights, even accounting for the thing's size, it should be dead or at least reeling from the amount of fire Grant had poured into it.

"Impact in five seconds, sir," Keogh shouted and started counting down. "Four...Three..."

Captain Nicholson looked about the bridge at his crew. He took pride in the fact that even with death bearing down on them, they stayed at their stations.

"Impact!" Keogh wailed as the Kraken struck the *Hercules*. The ship was hurled upwards out of the water even as her aft section was folded inward like the hood of a car meeting an immovable object at high speed.

Captain Nicholson was flung from his chair to the floor of the bridge. He heard Mr. Malkin grunt as the man's ribs were shattered, his chest hurled into the helm. Malkin toppled sideways from his chair to land next to where Captain Nicholson rested on his aching hands and knees.

A power surge shot through the *Hercules'* systems, blowing out just about every station on the bridge. Keogh died instantly as the sonar station blew apart in an explosion of flames and shrapnel. Grant threw himself away from the weapons station, narrowly avoiding the same fate.

The *Hercules* flopped back into the water, tossing her bridge officers about like ragged dolls, Captain Nicholson among them. Captain Nicholson had been trying to get back on his feet as the ship went down. Halfway up, he was hurled across the bridge to smash into the forward wall beneath the bridge window. His right shoulder took the brunt of the impact as he tried to brace himself. Captain Nicholson howled in pain as the shoulder was not only dislocated, but most of the bones inside it were crushed. Still, Captain Nicholson counted himself as lucky as he watched a crewman who was on fire rolling about on the floor of the bridge near its entrance.

"Grant!" Captain Nicholson yelled, stumbling to his feet. He clutched his shattered shoulder with his good hand, fighting not to black out from the pain.

His XO had made his way to the engineering console. "Rerouting weapon control now, sir!"

"Damage reports coming in from all over the ship, Captain," another crewman with shouted at him. The woman was using a handheld radio to communicate with the rest to the ship. *Now that was quick thinking*, Captain Nicholson admitted.

The *Hercules* shook again as the Kraken heaved a part of itself up onto the ship's forward deck. The giant beast's weight dragged the bow of the ship downward. Captain Nicholson grabbed the helm to keep his footing as the floor of the bridge titled. The helmsman, Malkin, looked up at him, his lips smeared with blood. "Hang in there, son," Captain Nicholson said, trying to comfort Malkin as he stepped over him, heading for the engineering station to join Grant there.

The rising body of the Kraken blocked out the starlight coming in through the bridge's forward window. The monster's burning yellow eyes were the only light that could be seen through it. Night had fallen as the battle raged on.

"I've got main gun control," Grant told him. "At least of the few guns we have left."

"Point blank to that thing's face," Captain Nicholson ordered.

"You know the blast will get us too," Grant said.

"We're dead anyway," Captain Nicholson replied. "Just do it."

"Yes, sir," Grant nodded.

Two of the *Hercules'* remaining 16-inch guns that were still functional swiveled on their mounts towards the Kraken as Grant guided them and locked them onto their target.

"It was an honor serving with you, sir," Grant said.

"The honor was mine," Captain Nicholson said, smiling at him. "Fire!"

The guns spat high-explosive shells directly into the Kraken. The ensuing explosion blew a good portion of the *Hercules* apart beneath the Kraken as they detonated. The massive beast released the *Hercules*, slipping into the waves as it leaked black blood from its freshly dealt wounds. Secondary explosions ripped along the length of the ship blowing bits of it skyward as smoke rolled from the blazing fires that danced on its deck. As the *Hercules* sank,

Captain Nicholson and Grant's bodies floated in the water that had come, racing into the bridge through its shattered forward window.

****

"The *Hercules* is gone, sir," Ennis reported.

Captain Weaver slumped in his command chair, feeling an odd mixture of grief and anger.

Smith, Watkins, Lancaster, and the rest of the *Braxton*'s bridge crew appeared to take the news just as hard. Miller, who had just taken over at the comm. station, ran the fingers of her right hand over her forehead, brushing hair from her eyes as she glanced over at him.

"Captain," Miller said to him, "the two doctors we brought aboard from the platform want to speak with you ASAP."

Captain Weaver nodded at Miller. "Tell them I'll be there as soon as I can."

"There's no sign of the Kraken, sir," Lancaster told him. "And we've put some distance between us and the lesser squid creatures."

"Thank you, Lancaster," Captain Weaver replied. "Mr. Ennis, you have command."

"Yes, sir," Ennis snapped, almost saluting him. Captain Weaver knew the stress was getting to them all.

Captain Weaver left the *Braxton*'s bridge, taking the shortest path to the medical bay where the two women were waiting on him. They had both checked out as being fine but had remained there anyway helping Dr. Hall with the ship's wounded as best they could. Though neither of them was truly a medical doctor, both were biologists, and Captain Weaver was sure that Dr. Hall was grateful for their help.

As soon as he entered the medical bay, they came running up to him.

"Is there somewhere we can talk in private?" Cheryl asked.

Captain Weaver motioned them into Dr. Hall's office and shut the door behind them.

"What's so urgent?" he demanded.

"Do you want to tell him?" Cheryl asked Dr. Bailey.

Dr. Bailey nodded and then dove into it. "We've been going over the reports your crew has filled in the ship's computer system about the *Braxton* and DESRON 2's engagements with the Kraken."

"And?" Captain Weaver pressed.

"We've come to the conclusion that the lesser squid creatures are indeed the Kraken's spawn and not just a symbiotic-like species acting in its defense," Cheryl told him.

"I don't see how that matters?" Captain Weaver shrugged, growing frustrated as he felt his time would be better spent on the *Braxton*'s bridge, monitoring the current situation and preparing to face the Kraken again. He had no delusion that Captain Nicholson, however capable the man was, had been able to destroy the monster alone. The Kraken would be coming from them next soon enough.

Dr. Bailey cleared her throat. "Captain Weaver, we believe that the Kraken is a female."

Captain Weaver was afraid he knew where Dr. Bailey was going and he was right.

"It's going to reproduce," Cheryl said.

"If it hasn't already," Dr. Bailey added.

"When it does, the number of eggs…" Cheryl paused. "They'll be enough to change the ecosystem of the Earth's oceans."

"One batch of eggs could do that?" Captain Weaver asked.

"When you're talking about thousands of creatures who will become the top of the food chain with no natural predator to stop their continued growth, yes," Dr. Bailey assured him.

"I see," Captain Weaver said, nodding. "And you're telling me this because?"

"Because you and this ship may be the only thing standing between that monster and utter dominance of the Earth's oceans," Cheryl stated.

"Look," Captain Weaver said, his voice hard, "I understand what you're saying, but battling sea monsters isn't my job right now. That thing just wiped out an entire DESRON. And DESRON 2 may have been labeled a DESRON, but she wasn't a real one. The ships she was composed of weren't destroyers. They were top-of-the-line battleships. The Kraken ripped through them so easily…"

"We're not saying it'll be easy," Cheryl pointed out. "But if we, you, don't stop the Kraken, and soon, we're talking about the fate of the planet here, Captain!"

"She's right, Captain Weaver," Dr. Bailey pleaded. "Can you imagine a world where the oceans are no longer mankind's? And worse, you've seen that the lesser squids are amphibious. There's nothing to prevent them from raiding or even claiming the coastal areas of the continents as their own. If this Kraken spawns a new generation of those lesser creatures, they alone will wreak havoc on this planet like nothing the human race has ever experienced before."

"And it's likely among the Kraken's eggs that there will be offspring that grow to like it as well. Surely, at least one, and that one, in turn, will spawn more until the creatures are multiplying a rate that even with all the technology and weapons the human race won't have a prayer of stopping them," Cheryl added.

Captain Weaver ran his fingers through his hair. He was still trying to process everything the two doctors had still told him when Dr. Hall decided to put in his two cents. Dr. Hall had been listening outside the door and opened it now to join them.

"You heard the ladies, Captain," Dr. Hall said. "No matter the cost, you don't have a choice. You have to stop this Kraken thing and stop it now."

"I don't suppose you brainiacs want to tell me how?" Captain Weaver snarled.

"You're the warrior, Captain Weaver." Dr. Bailey spread her hands wide in a show that she deferred to his experience in such matters.

"You should know that we believe the Kraken regenerates like a lizard that can grow back a cut off tail, only at a much accelerated rate," Cheryl told him. "We've been watching what we could of its fight with DESRON 2 through your ship's systems thanks to Dr. Hall. That's why the thing is still alive despite all the firepower that has been poured into it."

"Anything else?" Captain Weaver rasped.

"We think that in order to kill it, whatever you do is going need do so in a single strike. Due to its healing factor, just wounding it won't work. Instead of bleeding out like a normal animal would, it will simply heal itself," Dr. Bailey said.

"Great." Captain Weaver shot them a wry grin, his tone sarcastic. "I'll get right on figuring out how to kill that thing with a single hit. I imagine a tactical nuke would do the job nicely. Don't suppose you brought one onboard with you?"

The two women clearly didn't appreciate his dark humor.

"This is nothing to joke about, Captain," Cheryl told him. "The fate of the very world perhaps is in your hands."

"No pressure," Captain Weaver chuckled darkly. "No pressure at all."

"You'd best be getting back to the bridge." Dr. Hall laid a hand on his shoulder. "You've got to kill this thing, Captain. You're the only one who can in time and you know it."

"Right then." Captain Weaver nodded and gently removed Dr. Hall's hand. "Ladies," he said in parting and left the medical bay. As he walked along the corridor towards the lift that would take him to the bridge, his mind reeled at the staggering magnitude of the task ahead of him. He hoped Ennis would have an idea as for how to kill the Kraken in a single hit because he sure as Hades didn't.

****

Captain Weaver stepped onto the bridge, looking around at his crew as he did so.

"Captain on the bridge!" Mr. Smith snapped as he entered.

Ennis leaped out of his command chair, surrendering it to him.

Captain Weaver plopped in the chair and sighed.

"Sir?" Ennis asked. "Is everything okay?"

"No." Captain Weaver shook his head. He knew his crew was one of the best in the fleet. He trusted them with his life on a daily basis. It just made sense to fill them all in on what lay ahead of them and he did so in short order. When he was done, Ennis was staring at him.

"Killing that thing in a single hit is a pretty dang tall order, sir," Ennis said, echoing his own thoughts.

"I know," Captain Weaver replied, "but it sounds like it's up to us to do it. Even if the long-range comms were working, it's unlikely any help would arrive in time. If we don't find a means of stopping this thing, it's game over for us all." He said the last part in his best Bill Paxton voice.

"Don't you think that's a touch dramatic?" Ennis said.

"You've seen those things move about out of the water," Captain Weaver reminded his XO. "Can you imagine the effect creatures like that will have on fishing, shipping, small coastal towns? My God, man, we're really talking about the end of the world as we know it if that thing and its spawn aren't stopped."

Ennis stared at him in silence. It was Smith who spoke up.

"I think I have an idea, sir," Smith said, getting up from the weapons station, "but you're not going to like it."

"I'm listening," Captain Weaver said.

"We've seen how the Kraken deals with ships the size of the *Braxton*, sir." Smith spun around in his seat to look at him. "That thing… It comes right in and latches onto its target. Its tactic has been to crush the ship it is engaged with and then drag it underwater. What if we had a surprise waiting for it when it tried that against us?"

Captain Weaver stared at Smith. "Are you suggesting we sacrifice this ship to destroy that thing, Mr. Smith?"

"It's the only way I can think of killing it, Captain," Mr. Smith said honestly. "We have seen that normal tactics don't work. We just don't have the firepower to kill it in a single hit any other way."

"He's right," Ennis reluctantly admitted. "It may very well be the only means of stopping that thing."

"I'm not arguing that it wouldn't work," Captain Weaver replied with a sigh. "But allow me to remind you that the waters are teeming with the lesser squids. If we lure the Kraken in and blow the ship to kill it, what about them? The lifeboats aren't equipped for combat. Any crew who don't stay aboard will be left at their mercy."

"Not necessarily," Ennis said. "If the big one dies, the others may scatter. Its death might break them and send them running."

"That's a pretty risky gamble to take," Captain Weaver complained.

"I don't see how we have another choice, sir." Ennis shrugged. "Not if you really intend to try to kill the thing."

Captain Weaver thought it over and then nodded. "Mr. Smith, how long will it take to rig this ship for what you have in mind?"

"With enough manpower to help, maybe an hour?" Smith answered.

"Be about it then. Pull as many crewmen as you need to assist," Captain Weaver ordered. "Ennis, relieve him in the meantime."

"Yes, sir," Ennis replied, taking over the weapons station for Smith as the younger officer left the bridge.

"Lancaster?" Captain Weaver called out.

The sonar tech snapped to attention at his station. "Sir!"

"Any sign of the Kraken as yet?" Captain Weaver asked.

"None, sir," Lancaster reported. "I'm picking up a large number of the lesser squid creatures in pursuit of us though. They're hanging back for now but keeping their speed constant with our own."

"I want to know the second there is any change," Captain Weaver ordered him.

The *Braxton* had maintained action stations since the last engagement with the squids and the death of DESRON 2. Captain Weaver knew they were as ready as they could be should the Kraken show itself given their situation, except for putting in places the charges needed for Mr. Smith's plan. Lord willing, the Kraken would give the weapons officer the time to get everything in place before the monster showed itself again.

"Maintain current course and speed. We need to keep as much distance as we can from those things until Mr. Smith is ready." Captain Weaver leaned back in his chair. "And somebody get me a bloody cup of coffee!"

****

Lieutenant Commander Kim Unger had taken charge of the *Braxton*'s onboard marines and security personnel. She knew it was up to her and her men to keep the ship from being overrun by the lesser squid creatures should they move in ahead of the Kraken itself. All of the ship's entrances to its interior had been welded shut except for one passageway onto its primary deck, and those doors were now closed with two soldiers carrying SAWs in place to defend it. The rest of her men were spread out all along the sides of the *Braxton*, heavily armed and their eyes fixed on the waves for any sign of trouble.

Her second-in-command, Henson, came running over to where she stood at the portside railing.

"Ma'am," he shouted. "We've got reports of the squids moving in from both aft and starboard."

Unger blinked in surprise. She hadn't expected the squids to come calling already. "Have the men engage them at will."

As soon as she gave the order, a soldier a few yards up the deck from her shouted, "Contact from starboard!"

Lieutenant Commander Unger whirled back towards the water. What she saw there nearly made her freeze despite her years of experience and training. There were squid creatures everywhere among the waves, far too many of them to count at a glance. She jerked her rifle up, bracing it against her shoulder as she took aim at the monsters. Her first burst ripped the central mass of one of the things apart. Black blood swirled in the water around where its corpse floated, jostled about by the current. She took aim at another but didn't pull the trigger. Out of the corner of her eye, she noticed movement below her and to her right on the *Braxton*'s lower hull. The squid creatures had already reached the ship and were emerging from the water to climb its sides. She twisted her body to get a shot at one of the monsters already in the process of racing up the side of the ship like some sort of deranged spider on speed. Its tentacles lashed out, their spear-like tips thrusting into the metal of the *Braxton*'s hull as it used them to pull itself upwards. Lieutenant Commander Unger took aim at one the squids that was halfway up the side of the ship and put a burst of rounds into it. The squid creature gave a horrid, high-pitched shriek of pain and died where it was. Its body dangled from the side of the *Braxton* as the tentacles impaling the ship's hull held its corpse in place above the waves.

The first of the squids to reach the top of the *Braxton*'s starboard side hurled itself up and over the railing at one of her men. The poor bastard never stood a chance against it. He turned, trying to bring his rifle into play, but the squid was just too fast. Before his rifle was halfway around towards it, one of the thing's tentacles knocked his head from his shoulders in an explosion of blood. The man's head went rolling across the *Braxton*'s deck as his body toppled over. The man next to him fired into the squid, blowing it to pieces with a stream of automatic fire, only to die as another squid cleared the railing. It landed on his back, taking him to the deck below its madly writhing limbs. The man screamed as the creature's tentacles gutted him where he lay. Red slicked, purple strands of his intestines were thrown from his body and sprawled over the deck around him.

Lieutenant Commander Unger was caught off guard as a squid came bounding over the railing near her. She narrowly avoided the thing's tentacle that lashed outward towards her throat. The squid creature landed on the deck facing her. Leveling her rifle at its central mass, she sent it to help with a trio of quick bursts. It flopped over to lay still as black blood pooled about its corpse. She turned and started to yell an order at Henson only to find him dead. His cut-up and broken body rested on the deck a few feet away. Two of the squid creatures squatted like alien tripods over it, shoveling bits of his flesh and organs into their maws. Unger felt vomit and bile rise up in her throat, but she fought them down. If she bent over to puke up her last meal, the squids would tear her apart like they had her second-in-command. Cursing herself as she ran, Lieutenant Commander Unger abandoned her position and sprinted towards the only entrance left to the *Braxton*'s interior deck. The ship's CIWS had fallen silent. The squids must have taken it out somehow, but she had no time to check on it. Her life depended on her speed.

"Fall back!" she shouted as she raced towards the two troopers guarding the doorway ahead of her, being careful to stay out of their line of fire. The few men who were still alive on the part of the *Braxton*'s deck she was on fell in behind her as her legs pumped beneath her. Her breath came in ragged gasps, her body pushed to its limits and then some.

One of the door guards swept the arc of fire from his SAW over a mass of squid creatures advancing towards the door from the port side of the ship. The bullets tore into their forward ranks, severing tentacles, rupturing flesh, and filling the air with sprays of black blood. Dozens of the squid creatures died in the barrage of fire, but for each that fell, another took its place. Taking a quick look around her as she continued to run, Lieutenant Commander Unger yelled, "Close the doors! Close the doors now!"

She knew doing so would seal her fate and those of her remaining men as well, but if the squid creatures got into the corridors of the ship's interior, it would all be over. Better they gave their lives to save those inside the ship than for everyone to be lost.

The larger of the two guards dropped his SAW and moved towards the doorway's control pad. He finished his work, the heavy doors beginning to slide closed, as she reached him.

"Pick up your weapon, soldier," Unger snapped at him. "You're going need it!"

The big man retrieved his SAW and rejoined the fight as Unger and the other guard fired in the squids closing in on them. Her other soldiers who had been retreating towards the doorway in her wake were all dead. The squid creatures had overtaken them and littered the deck with their ripped and broken bodies. *It was just the three of them now*, Unger thought, *but they would hold out as long as they could.* They had to buy Captain Weaver the time he needed to deal with the squids or the rest of her men would have all died in vain.

A heavy SAW chattered and thundered to each side of her as Unger held the trigger of her rifle tight, emptying what was left of its magazine into the charging squids. As her rifle clicked empty, the squids reached her and the doorway's two guards. The big man to her right was lifted from his feet as the spear-like tip of a tentacle entered his ribs and flung his bleeding form about like an angry child shaking a ragged doll. The man to her left cried out in the moment before the tip of a tentacle pierced his skull through his right eye and its tip emerged from the back of his head in an explosion of brain matter, blood, and bone fragments. Lieutenant Commander Unger threw her empty rifle at a squid which leaped at her, its tentacles reaching out to take her into their hold. The impact of the weapon changed the angle of the squid creature's leap just enough for her to dodge its groping tentacles as she yanked her sidearm free from the holster on her hip. The squid had landed next to her and was already in the process of whirling about as she rammed the barrel of the pistol into its open, shrieking mouth and squeezed the trigger four times in rapid succession. The bullets ripped through what passed for the squid's head, killing the thing instantly. Unger kicked its corpse away from as she spun to fire a trio of shots at another squid charging at her. Each shot hit the squid, digging into its flesh, but the 9mm rounds just didn't have the stopping power to save her.

A tentacle took grasped each of her arms and pulled them away from her body. Unger howled in pain as she felt her muscles tearing beneath her skin. Another tentacle jutted towards her. It rammed itself through her throat, severing the top of her spinal column at the base of her neck in the process. The squid creature jerked her already dead body closer to it as its mouth stretched open in anticipation of the taste of her blood.

****

"Do it," Captain Weaver ordered Ennis. He had been monitoring the battle on the deck and knew that Lieutenant Commander Unger and her men were dead. The crew needed to be evacuated before the Kraken showed up, and that couldn't be done with a legion of squid creatures swarming on her the deck.

Before the lieutenant commander and her men had taken up their defensive positions and the attack by the squid creatures had begun, Captain Weaver had instructed her to place charges along the length of the *Braxton*. The charges were all incendiary in nature, designed so that they wouldn't hurt the structure of the ship. Flames could scorch the metal of her walls without actually damaging them. The plan was to use those charges to clear the deck should the lieutenant commander and her men fail.

His XO, Ennis, stabbed the button to detonate the charges. The deck of the *Braxton* lit up a burst of flame that ripped through the squid creatures, cooking them where they were. In its wake, the deck was littered with the burnt and smoking remains of their bodies.

"The deck is clear, sir," Ennis reported.

"All non-essential personnel, abandon ship," Captain Weaver said over the *Braxton*'s internal comm. system. "I repeat, all non-essential personnel, abandon ship."

"How's the water out there, Mr. Lancaster?" Captain Weaver asked.

"Mostly clear, sir," Lancaster answered. "Almost all of the lesser squid creatures were aboard us when the charges detonated."

"Good." Captain Weaver leaned forward in his command chair, teetering on its edge.

Not a single member of his bridge crew had chosen to leave. He was proud of them for their courage and thankful because he was about to need the skills of each and every one of them.

"Any sign of the Kraken?" Captain Weaver glanced over at Lancaster.

"None yet, sir," the sonar tech answered.

The seconds ticked by like hours as Captain Weaver watched the bulk of the *Braxton*'s crew scurrying to her lifeboats and getting them into the water. Though it felt like the evacuation took an eternity, it actually took less than fifteen minutes. When the final lifeboat was away, Captain Weaver slid back fully into his chair and motioned at his helmsmen. "Alter course back the way we came. Let's put as much distance between us and those boats as you can before the big one comes calling. Maximum military power."

"Aye, aye, sir," came the reply.

The massive battleship came about in the water, her engines pushed to their limits. Captain Weaver wasn't waiting for the Kraken to come to them anymore. He was planning on running straight down the blasted thing's throat.

The *Braxton*'s CIWS had been damaged in the battle on the deck between the lieutenant commander's men and the lesser squids. Not having its firepower to be added to the ship's main guns wasn't as much as of a problem as it could have been, considering what Captain Weaver had planned for the Kraken.

"Contact, sir!" Lancaster shouted, nearly leaping out of his seat at the sonar station. "It's the Kraken!"

"Where?" Captain Weaver snapped.

"The Kraken is coming in at an angle on our starboard side captain. CBDR at forty knots. It looks like it's going to attempt to ram us, sir," Lancaster reported.

"We can't have that now, can we?" Captain Weaver smirked. "Mr. Smith, slow the mother down some if you would."

"With pleasure, sir." Mr. Smith grinned, happy to be back at the weapons station again. He had taken it over from Ennis as soon as the surprises scattered through the ship had been put in place for the Kraken.

The *Braxton*'s main guns locked on the fast-approaching monster and thundered as they opened fire on it. The sixteen guns spat high-explosion shells into the monster. Water mixed with black blood splashed skyward as they impacted the Kraken.

Watching the data scrolling on the small screen of the arm of his command chair, Captain Weaver could see that the Kraken wasn't as fast or agile as it had been. The great beast likely hadn't fully healed from the last engagement yet. That was a very good thing. It slowed even more as the heavy shells continued to strike it and explode.

"The Kraken is slowing, sir!" Lancaster called out. "It's still on course for us though."

As crazy as the desperate plan that he, Smith, and Ennis had come up with was, Captain Weaver was really beginning to believe it just might work. "That's right. Keep coming, you bastard," he muttered under his breath. Smith had placed enough charges along the length of the ship to blow it into oblivion several times over, and that wasn't even taking into account the ship's ordnance, which would surely be set off by the explosion of those charges as well. The Kraken might think it was dragging them into the depths, but in truth, they'd be taking it to Hell with them.

"Impact in five!" Lancaster shouted.

"Brace for it," Captain Weaver had just enough time to order before the Kraken slammed into the battleship's starboard side. The impact nearly flung Captain Weaver from his seat. If he hadn't braced himself by clutching the command chair's arms, it would have. None of the rest of the bridge crew suffered anything worse than being jostled about either.

"Damage report!" Captain Weaver yelled.

"We're taking on water, sir!" Ennis answered him. "The starboard side hull has been breached. Main power is still online but down by thirty-six percent."

The report was a lot better than Captain Weaver had expected it to be. Thank God the great beast hadn't hit any vital systems or they would be in a lot more trouble than they were.

Captain Weaver started to ask Lancaster and Ennis if the Kraken had taken their bait, but the bridge shook again as one of the monster's impossibly long tentacles rose into the air only to fall back onto the *Braxton*. It coiled about the ship, wrapping over and under it. A second tentacle joined the first moment later. The Kraken was too close in now to use the main guns without them inflicting as much if not more damage to the ship herself if they fired at the creature. That didn't matter though. Captain Weaver had the Kraken right where he wanted it.

****

Hawks, along with Robbie and Hyatt, had been tasked with making sure that Cheryl and Bailey made it safely away from the *Braxton*. A newbie soldier named Jeff had joined their squad for the effort. Hawks felt strange being in a command. It wasn't something he had ever sought or wanted, but with Larson dead, it had fallen onto his shoulders. The four of them had rushed the two women through the burning bodies of the squid creatures on the *Braxton*'s deck and onto a motorized lifeboat.

Hyatt and the newbie kept an eye out for more of the lesser squid creatures in the water as he sat in the boat's center with the two women. Robbie had his tablet hooked up to the *Braxton*'s systems and watched its screen intently, monitoring the situation behind them as the lifeboat bounced across the waves at its highest possible speed. The idea was to put as much distance between them and the battle that was about to take place as quickly as they could. All their hope lay in Captain Weaver being able to take out the Kraken and the lesser squids scattering in panic upon the great beast's death.

Robbie had plotted them a course northward towards the closest high-traffic shipping lane. Hawks knew that Robbie hoped once the Kraken was dead that the EM interference with the long-range comm. gear would clear up, and he'd simply be able to radio for help. Failing that, the boat carried enough supplies for them to hold for a while and pray that another ship passing through the area would pick them up, assuming of course that the lesser squid creatures didn't come after them. If they did, the boat had no weapons, and Hawks knew that the amount of time they'd be able to hold off the creatures would be a very short one. He and his men had loaded up on weapons and ammo before leaving the *Braxton*, but in the water, the squid creatures had the advantage. Even if they could keep the things from getting onto the small boat or being pulled from it by the things, the squid creatures could easily use their numbers to flip the boat over. If they did, that would be game over for them all.

Hawks knew how important Cheryl and Bailey were. Both of them were scientists, and Cheryl had been in charge of the platform crew that had discovered the Kraken. It was essential that they survived and made it home. If Captain Weaver failed to kill the Kraken, the powers that be would need every scrap of information that the two women could provide them with about the great beast. Even if Captain Weaver succeeded, there would still be the lesser squid creatures out there to be mopped up and dealt with. From what he had overheard the two doctors telling Robbie about the things, they weren't as big of a threat as the Kraken itself was, but that wasn't to say that the things couldn't breed among themselves given time. Hawks understood that was the main fear. He didn't even want to think about what would happen if the monsters were allowed to breed and took over the planet's oceans, as they surely would with no modern-day predators to hold them in check. Humanity would find itself at war with the creatures for the control of the oceans, and Hawks didn't think for a second that it would be a fair fight. All of mankind's tech and weapons might give them an edge in the beginning, but if the squid creatures multiplied as quickly as Cheryl and Bailey claimed they might, the edge would be quickly lost. No shipping lane would be safe from the things. Worse, with how they were able to move about and breathe out of the water, most coastal cities and towns would likely find themselves being swarmed by the monsters once their numbers increased.

Shaking his head as if to clear his thoughts, Hawks looked over at Hyatt. "We clear?"

"So far." Hyatt smiled at him.

"Stay sharp," Hawks ordered Hyatt and Jeff.

"Yes, sir," Jeff snapped at him.

Hawks had to suppress a grin at the young man's over eagerness to come across as professional.

"Mr. Hawks," Dr. Bailey said, "I hope you don't believe your men will truly be able to spot the creatures if they don't want to be seen."

"We have to try, ma'am." Hawks shrugged. "It's our job. Our lives could all depend on spotting those things far enough out to pump some fire into them before they get close enough to be a threat."

"If they truly want us, they'll have us no matter you do," Cheryl said.

"I would rather not think about that, ma'am," Hawks replied.

The small boat's motor roared as it continued to put distance between itself and the *Braxton*. Hawks had taken over guiding the boat from Cheryl once they were fully underway. The woman impressed him. Both of them did. These ladies were tough for being scientists and knew their way around boats and the water as well as himself or any of his men.

"We have just got to have faith that we're going to make it home alive," Hawks added.

****

Metal screamed as it bent inward and tore apart. The Kraken had a tight hold around the *Braxton* and had started the process of crushing the battleship. The bridge continued to shake as the Kraken vented its wrath upon the *Braxton*. Several small fires burned on stations that had shorted out from the damage the monster had done to the ship. The bridge stank of smoke and burning wires.

It still blew Captain Weaver's mind that such a creature could exist as he watched it through the bridge's shattered forward window. To think that any type of animal could go head to head with modern battleships and win was scary as hell. If he lived through this, Captain Weaver knew he would give up his command and walk away from his career. Even then, nightmares of the beast would haunt him for the rest of his life. Thankfully, he didn't plan on living through this mess. He intended to go out in a blaze of glory, taking the monster with him. All of what was happening would likely be given the highest level of classification, but if the details of all that had happened here were released some distance time in the future, he couldn't help but wonder what the history books would say about him. A smile crept over his lips as he thought, *Captain Weaver, monster slayer.*

"We're taking on heavy water through the damage on the starboard side, sir!" Ennis called to him.

Thankfully, the bulk of the crew had been evacuated before the battle started, and everyone who had opted to stay aboard had done so of their own freewill. Causalities were no longer something he needed to worry about or feel guilt over. Everyone who had stayed had accepted their fate and knew that death lay ahead of them.

"Helm control is gone, sir," Watkins told him.

"Doesn't matter." Captain Weaver continued to smile. "That thing isn't letting us go now that it's got us."

Captain Weaver leaned back into his command chair. "Mr. Ennis, would you do the honor?"

One of the Kraken's impossibly large, yellow eyes moved in front of the bridge's window. Captain Weaver stared into it. Its gaze chilled him to the bone. There was an intelligence behind it that was both cold and alien. He imagined the monster saw him much as he would an insect and merely something to be crushed beneath. Staring into that giant eye and seeing the evil, as man would define it, there, Captain Weaver was ready to give his life to end the thing.

"Any time you're ready, Mr. Ennis," Captain Weaver urged.

"Activating charges now, sir," Ennis told him. "In three... two..."

Captain Weaver looked around the bridge at his crew, pride swelling within him at the sight of them. They were all so brave and they were about to save the entire the world.

"One," Mr. Ennis said and hit the button that detonated the charges Mr. Smith had placed through the length of the *Braxton*. All of the charges went off simultaneously in a single massive blast that blew the massive battleship apart. Captain Weaver died in a flash of light and heat that burned the skin from his bones.

The Kraken never knew what it hit. One second it was clinging to its prey, the *Braxton* crippled and helpless in its tentacles. The next, its prey became a mass of fire and metal that burned and ripped at its body. The great beast died like a soldier who had thrown himself on top of a grenade. Pieces of the *Braxton* blew their way through its flesh, leaving jagged, bleeding holes in their wake. The Kraken's corpse slid off the *Braxton*, sinking into the waves, turning the water black with its blood.

****

The explosion that destroyed the *Braxton* was so powerful and loud that Hawks and those who shared the small boat under his command with him heard it despite the distance and the roar of the boat's pushed to its limit motor. The flash of the explosion lit up the distant horizon beneath the clear night sky.

"The *Braxton* is gone, sir," Robbie told him.

"And the Kraken?" Hawks asked.

Robbie had his tablet tapped into the ship's systems and had been able to monitor the last bits of information that they had picked up before being destroyed along with the ship.

"As best I can tell, sir, Captain Weaver's plan worked." Robbie smiled. "The monster is dead."

Hyatt let out a victory whoop, nearly leaping up from where he sat at the portside edge of the small lifeboat. The newbie, Jeff, was smiling too.

"The nightmare is finally over," Hawks muttered under his breath.

"That's yet to be seen," Cheryl reminded him sharply.

"Hyatt, Jeff," Hawks said. "Are we clear?"

"No sign of the squids, sir," Hyatt answered.

"Then we'll just have to hope they're gone too," Hawks growled. He kept the small lifeboat's motor at its max and steered it onward towards the coordinates of the shipping lane Robbie had set their course for.

Hawks said a silent prayer for the souls of those who had given their lives aboard the *Braxton*, turning his gaze upwards to the stars. His rifle rested on the floor of the boat next to him. He hoped that he wouldn't need to use it. Cheryl was right though; only time would tell if the nightmare was truly over. But for now, they were safe and headed home.

END

Author Bio

Eric S Brown is the author of numerous book series including the Bigfoot War series, the Kaiju Apocalypse series (with Jason Cordova), the Crypto-Squad series (with Jason Brannon), the Homeworld series (With Tony Faville and Jason Cordova), the Jack Bunny Bam series, and the A Pack of Wolves series. Some of his stand alone books include Dropship Marines, Kraken, Operation Hive Strike, The Last Fleet, War of the Worlds plus Blood Guts and Zombies, World War of the Dead, Last Stand in a Dead Land, Sasquatch Lake, Kaiju Armageddon, Megalodon, Megalodons, and Megalodon Apocalypse to name only a few. His short fiction has been published hundreds of times in the small press in beyond including markets like the Onward Drake and Black Tide Rising anthologies from Baen Books, the Grantville Gazette, the SNAFU Military horror anthology series, and Walmart World magazine. He has done the novelizations for such films as Boggy Creek: The Legend is True (Studio 3 Entertainment) and The Bloody Rage of Bigfoot (Great Lake films). The first book of his Bigfoot War series was adapted into a feature film by Origin Releasing in 2014. Werewolf Massacre at Hell's Gate was the second his books to be adapted into film in 2015. In addition to his fiction, Eric also writes an award winning comic book news column entitled "Comics in a Flash" and ongoing series of stories about a group of live action roleplaying teens for the Grantville Gazette set in Eric Flint's world of *1632*. Eric lives in North Carolina with his wife and two children where he continues to write tales of the hungry dead, blazing guns, and the things that lurk in the woods.

CHECK OUT OTHER GREAT DEEP SEA THRILLERS

LAMPREYS
by Alan Spencer

A secret government tactical team is sent to perform a clean sweep of a private research installation. Horrible atrocities lurk within the abandoned corridors. Mutated sea creatures with insane killing abilities are waiting to suck the blood and meat from their prey.

Unemployed college professor Conrad Garfield is forced to assist and is soon separated from the team. Alone and afraid, Conrad must use his wits to battle mutated lampreys, infected scientists and go head-to-head with the biggest monstrosity of all.

Can Conrad survive, or will the deadly monsters suck the very life from his body?

DEEP DEVOTION
by M.C. Norris

Rising from the depths, a mind-bending monster unleashes a wave of terror across the American heartland. Kate Browning, a Kansas City EMT confronts her paralyzing fear of water when she traces the source of a deadly parasitic affliction to the Gulf of Mexico. Cooperating with a marine biologist, she travels to Florida in an effort to save the life of one very special patient, but the source of the epidemic happens to be the nest of a terrifying monster, one that last rose from the depths to annihilate the lost continent of Atlantis.

Leviathan, destroyer, devoted lifemate and parent, the abomination is not going to take the extermination of its brood well.

CHECK OUT OTHER GREAT
DEEP SEA THRILLERS

PREDATOR X
by C.J Waller

When deep level oil fracking uncovers a vast subterranean sea, a crack team of cavers and scientists are sent down to investigate. Upon their arrival, they disappear without a trace. A second team, including sedimentologist Dr Megan Stoker, are ordered to seek out Alpha Team and report back their findings. But Alpha team are nowhere to be found – instead, they are faced with something unexpected in the depths. Something ancient. Something huge. Something dangerous. Predator X

DEAD BAIT
by Tim Curran

A husband hell-bent on revenge hunts a Wereshark...A Russian mail order bride with a fishy secret...Crabs with a collective consciousness...A vampire who transforms into a Candiru...Zombie piranha...Bait that will have you crawling out of your skin and more. Drawing on horror, humor with a helping of dark fantasy and a touch of deviance, these 19 contemporary stories pay homage to the monsters that lurk in the murky waters of our imaginations. If you thought it was safe to go back in the water...Think Again!

CHECK OUT OTHER GREAT
DEEP SEA THRILLERS

MEGA
by Jake Bible

There is something in the deep. Something large. Something hungry. Something prehistoric.
And Team Grendel must find it, fight it, and kill it.
Kinsey Thorne, the first female US Navy SEAL candidate has hit rock bottom. Having washed out of the Navy, she turned to every drink and drug she could get her hands on. Until her father and cousins, all ex-Navy SEALS themselves, offer her a way back into the life: as part of a private, elite combat Team being put together to find and hunt down an impossible monster in the Indian Ocean. Kinsey has a second chance, but can she live through it?

THE BLACK
by Paul E Cooley

Under 30,000 feet of water, the exploration rig Leaguer has discovered an oil field larger than Saudi Arabia, with oil so sweet and pure, nations would go to war for the rights to it. But as the team starts drilling exploration well after exploration well in their race to claim the sweet crude, a deep rumbling beneath the ocean floor shakes them all to their core. Something has been living in the oil and it's about to give birth to the greatest threat humanity has ever seen.

"The Black" is a techno/horror-thriller that puts the horror and action of movies such as Leviathan and The Thing right into readers' hands. Ocean exploration will never be the same."